PRAISE FOR RACHEL VAN DYKEN

"*The Consequence of Loving Colton* is a must-read friends-to-lovers story that's as passionate and sexy as it is hilarious!"

—Melissa Foster, *New York Times* bestselling author

"Just when you think Van Dyken can't possibly get any better, she goes and delivers *The Consequence of Loving Colton*. Full of longing and breathless moments, this is what romance is about."

—Lauren Layne, *USA Today* bestselling author

"The tension between Milo and Colton made this story impossible to put down. Quick, sexy, witty—easily one of my favorite books from Rachel Van Dyken."

—R. S. Grey, *USA Today* bestselling author

"Hot, funny . . . will leave you wishing you could get marked by one of the immortals!"

—Molly McAdams, *New York Times* bestselling author, on *The Dark Ones*

"Laugh-out-loud fun! Rachel Van Dyken is on my auto-buy list."

—Jill Shalvis, *New York Times* bestselling author, on *The Wager*

"*The Dare* is a laugh-out-loud read that I could not put down. Brilliant. Just brilliant."

—Cathryn Fox, *New York Times* bestselling author

Kickin' It

The Seaside Series

Tear
Pull
Shatter
Forever
Fall
Eternal
Strung
Capture

The Renwick House Series

The Ugly Duckling Debutante
The Seduction of Sebastian St. James
An Unlikely Alliance
The Redemption of Lord Rawlings
The Devil Duke Takes a Bride

The London Fairy Tales Series

Upon a Midnight Dream
Whispered Music
The Wolf's Pursuit
When Ash Falls

The Seasons of Paleo Series

Savage Winter
Feral Spring

The Wallflower Series (with Leah Sanders)

Waltzing with the Wallflower
Beguiling Bridget
Taming Wilde

The Dark Ones Saga

The Dark Ones
Untouchable Darkness
Dark Surrender
Darkest Temptation

Stand-Alones

Hurt: A Collection (with Kristin Vayden and Elyse Faber)
Rip
Compromising Kessen
Every Girl Does It
The Parting Gift (with Leah Sanders)
Divine Uprising

Kickin' It

Red Card, Book Two

RACHEL VAN DYKEN

SKYSCAPE

SKYSCAPE

Text copyright © 2019 by Rachel Van Dyken
All rights reserved.

Published by Skyscape, New York

www.apub.com

Amazon, the Amazon logo, and Skyscape are trademarks of Amazon.com, Inc., or its affiliates.

ISBN-13: 9781542006606
ISBN-10: 1542006600

Cover design by Letitia Hasser

Cover photography by Wander Aguiar Photography

Printed in the United States of America

To my husband, who spent countless hours ordering takeout so I could finish this book. Love you, babe!

Chapter One

Matt

"No," I said firmly as my sister, Willow, tried to speak over me.

"But Matt, I—"

"No." I yawned and stared out across the pier. Paradise. I lived in paradise. All the hard work, all the blood, sweat, tears, all the whiny athletes I represented and insane hours, it had all paid off, hadn't it? I was living in a mansion overlooking the Puget Sound with my own infinity pool and hot tub just footsteps away from my master bedroom. I was happy.

I had everything.

A twinge of something hit me in the chest. I ignored it. The cool ocean breeze stung my face as my sister sighed on the other end of the phone like I was the one being unreasonable.

I loved the little pain in the ass.

She was smart.

Manipulative.

And almost impossible to say no to. Which was why I tried to keep her argument to a minimum; hell, I'd just say no until my voice went hoarse.

It was my fault. I'd been too protective of her when we were kids, and after our parents' death I'd taken raising her almost too seriously.

Making sure she knew right from wrong. I didn't realize I was making a carbon copy of myself until she started showing interest in every single thing I did. I could at least be thankful it was the positive things like holding down a job and not doping to get ahead in the league.

I shuddered as guilt settled on my shoulders. Guilt that staying in the league had been so important I'd completely forgotten my morals.

My breath hitched as disappointment swiftly replaced that guilt, because on days like this, I did miss it. I rubbed my chest as an ache started to form dead center; I missed the crowd yelling my name. I'd been a good player, but I was a better agent.

"Matt."

"Willow."

"Two chocolate cakes, one peanut-butter-fudge sundae, and Starbucks delivered to you every morning."

My eye twitched. I'd officially created a monster. "Two weeks?"

"One."

"I'm listening." My mouth watered. Damn her for knowing every weakness I possessed and using it against me.

She took a deep breath. "I majored in business."

I tried not to sound too annoyed at her obvious information dump. "I'm aware."

"Stop interrupting me."

"Sorry." I pinched the bridge of my nose and sat on the edge of one of the wicker chairs as the breeze picked up around me. I had a million things I'd rather be doing than listening to my sister list all the reasons it was a good idea for her to join an agency and rep athletes.

"As I was saying," she huffed, "I majored in business. I went to the school you chose for me because I trust you. I majored in something safe even though my heart wasn't in it. I played soccer just like you, I graduated summa cum laude just like you—"

"Is there a point to this?"

"Yes!" She sounded like she wanted to reach through the phone and strangle me. "I've followed in your footsteps because I admire you—and I think if you look at it logically you'll come to the same conclusion I have."

"That I did everything better?" I wondered out loud.

"My ass," she snorted. "You know I want to go into the family business—I want to manage athletes."

"Ah, this again."

"Yes, this again!"

I suppressed a sigh. I loved her, and I was so damn proud of the woman she'd turned into. My lack of enthusiasm had nothing to do with her abilities, and everything to do with the fact that she was drop-dead gorgeous. Just the thought of her working around men who thought with their dicks at least 90 percent of the time had me ready to go to prison. Did I think she could handle it? Yes. Did imagining her working with any of the guys from the Bellevue Bucks still keep me up at night? Absolutely. She wasn't just my family, she was my only family, and I wanted to protect her from guys who thought nothing about one-night stands and dropping millions on a boat just because they could afford to—not that boats were a bad thing, I just didn't like guys who showed their worth with how much money they could spend.

Unable to hold it back any longer, I let out a frustrated sigh. "Willow."

"Stop saying my name as if it's going to calm me down. If anything, it just reminds me that you still treat me like a kid because the fact that I have boobs scares you!"

"I'm not scared of your boo—" I cut myself off because hadn't I just been thinking along those lines? Why couldn't I lock her in her room? Send her to Siberia? "Can we not talk about this now?"

"We're talking about it now!" she said a little forcefully. "I want to do something I love, something competitive and exciting. It's your

3

fault I fell in love with sports in the first place. I want to learn from the person I love the most in this world."

"Lay it on thicker and you'll suffocate yourself, Will."

She groaned. "My proposal is this: give me the summer to learn the ropes from your company. I swear I'll be great! It's impossible to get into this business without connections. You're my connection! And once the summer ends, you either hire me, or I'll look for something else."

"Uh-huh." I checked my watch and tried to ignore how sound her logic was, then checked my watch again. Damn, I was going to be late. "Look, you live in California, what are you going to do? Pack up all your shit, move here, and just . . . try it out? What if it doesn't work? You realize this is a huge commitment. You'll be around professional athletes who think their shit smells like roses. You have to be tough, you can't be . . . you," I coughed out. She was naturally flirtatious, and I could only imagine what some of my clients would think about that. "Sorry, that came out wrong."

"I'll prove myself," she said in a small whisper. "It's what I've always wanted, to be just like you."

"Ah, she offers cake while a knife gets shoved into my back. Nice." I let out a long sigh. I knew my reasons for saying no were purely out of fear, and maybe a little bit about her growing up too fast. "I'll give you three months."

"Yes!"

I pulled the phone away from my ear. "One catch. I'm not letting you just . . . live in a crappy apartment with no security where any of the athletes can track you, or downtown near the party scene. If you commit to this and—"

She burst out laughing. "Matt, do you hear yourself? Why would a professional athlete follow me to my crappy apartment? They aren't criminals! Or stalkers!"

I thought about some of my clients and winced. "Right . . ."

"Matt, be reasonable."

"You'll live here or the deal's off."

"Matt . . . I have a friend that's moving up there too, we were going to live—"

"Look, I gotta go. I'm running really late, you got what you want, congratulations. Send me the details later. I'm not trying to be an ass. If you want the job bad enough, you'll make it work."

"But what about—"

"Your friend will be fine. I really need to go, Jagger's waiting—"

"I mean I guess she could come with me."

"Sure! Yup. Sounds good." The clock was ticking in my head. There wasn't enough time in the world to babysit another athlete hell-bent on ruining his own reputation. "Whatever."

"Really?" she said.

What the hell was she talking about now? Was she still on the phone?

"Sure. Willow, I have to go. Love you, just put everything having to do with the move on the card, keep your receipts, and text me when you have details, yeah?"

"Matt, you're the best, I can't wait to tell—"

"Yeah, yeah, yeah, love you!"

I hung up and ran into my living room just in time to hear the doorbell. The door opened a few moments later.

"Yes, please, come in." I waved my arm in the air. "Jagger, you need to learn about boundaries, personal space . . ." I eyed his orange joggers. "Fashion . . ."

He rolled his eyes. "This is from one of my sponsors. I have to wear this shit so they pay me so I can pay you." He grinned.

"If I go blind from those pants I want a raise."

He flipped me off in typical Jagger style. The guy was one of soccer's highest-paid goalies and talked a lot of shit, but he did a good job taking it as well. He'd recently gotten into a verbal altercation with another player. As luck would have it, he was shoved into the ref and accidently gave him a black eye.

The video went viral.

It was his third viral video this year. He kept going viral for all the wrong reasons.

Keeping Jagger out of the news was an art.

Like swimming through shark-infested waters with a flesh wound . . . and surviving.

"So." Jagger plopped down onto my couch, taking up double the space needed to sit like a normal person. "What's the plan?"

I had opened my mouth to reply when the doorbell rang again.

The door opened before it stopped ringing.

Slade Rodriguez, best striker in the world, yawned and made his way toward Jagger.

"Why ring the doorbell if you never give me a chance to answer it?" I said louder than necessary.

Slade grinned. "Saw Jagger's car, figured he already made sure you weren't in your kitchen naked again."

I glared. "One time. And when a man lives by himself—"

"He tends to dance naked to John Legend?" Slade said while Jagger choked out a laugh.

I greedily started searching for my painkillers. With my luck, these two were going to give me a stomach ulcer at age thirty.

"Think he's already searching for ibuprofen?" Jagger whispered.

"It's all a front. We don't really bother him that much," Slade offered in a hushed tone. "Besides, he'd be bored without us."

"Actually . . ." I found a glass of water and threw back the pills in a big gulp. "The headache started when Willow called and wore me down to the point of complete exhaustion. She should have been a lawyer."

At my sister's name Jagger's eyes lit up. "Is this the hot one?"

"He only has one sister, dumbass." Slade laughed. "And she's really pretty, don't you think, Matt?"

I shook my head in dismay. Damn it, Slade had thrown me under the bus. I couldn't *not* compliment my own sister, but commenting on her just drew more attention to the fact that the woman could be a supermodel if she wanted. She wasn't even here and already I was breaking out in a cold sweat thinking about all the testosterone she'd be around on a daily basis. I had two female clients, the rest were men.

Slade I didn't worry about, he was in love. He was married.

Jagger, however, was single.

And ever since Slade had cleaned up his act, Jagger had just gotten worse, fighting with other players, sleeping around with girls who had big mouths and dollar signs in their eyes. His actions were either a cry for help or this was just who he was.

"She's . . . beautiful." I settled on *beautiful* because *pretty* sounded too interesting, *hot* sounded weird, and *sexy*, well, no, just no. "And completely off-limits—Jagger."

He held up his hands in surrender. "Hey, it's not my fault women come at me with their mouths open and shirts off—I call it the Jag effect."

"Something's wrong with you"—I narrowed my eyes at him— "besides the obvious character flaws the media seems to be gnawing on like a fucking bone." I loved the guy. I did. I'd been friends with him for years, but putting out his fires was getting exhausting.

"Oh, that's why I'm here." Slade raised his hand. "I figured we could do another charity game or something and put Jagger back in the spotlight in a positive way that helps the community." He grinned like he'd just gotten an A for awesome.

"Riiiight, let's just put the Jag effect out there for all to see and record and upload to YouTube . . ." I scowled. Even though that plan had worked before, we needed a different angle this time, and nothing screamed "good guy" more than family, and I knew just the woman to keep him in line. "You're taking your grandma to dinner."

Jagger paled, and Slade almost fell off the couch laughing.

"Anything but that," Jagger pleaded. "Look, I'll go paint houses, I'll build a fucking school!"

"It's just dinner." I smiled knowingly—I'd been on the opposite end of that woman's lectures more times than I could count.

"That's like saying it was just the Cold War." He glared. "She's very, very Russian, and she's loud, and last time she used a racial slur that almost got us kicked out of the restaurant."

"But she looks adorable, and if she starts getting loud be a big boy and stop her." I shot him an evil grin. "And people loved it when you held her hand in the parking lot. Those shots went viral."

"Right, about that: She asked me to hold her hand because she thought the police were following us because she used to date a Russian spy. Then she turned to me and asked, 'Or am I the spy?'" Jagger shuddered. "Matt, she talked into her wrist every few minutes like she was the KGB!"

"Take her out. Make it public. I don't care if she *is* a fucking spy, you strap her in that car of yours and take her out, you kiss her on the cheek, you pay for the bill, and when all is said and done, they'll post about how sweet it was that you were out with your grandma and not at some seedy bar signing autographs and picking out girls from a line."

"Once." He raised a forefinger. "And I was drunk. It was the only way I could decide which one was prettier."

"Yeah, I have to agree with Matt about Grandma," Slade said with a nod. "Also, stay far, far away from Willow."

"I love the name Willow." Jagger stared me down.

"I have no problem shoving you off my yacht and dumping a bucket of blood in afterward for good measure."

"Graphic." Jagger grinned. "I like it."

Slade stood. "What's for lunch?"

"You aren't staying for lunch."

"I'll get the plates!" Jagger followed.

I sighed and gave up. I was physically tired and mentally exhausted. These guys knew they could give me shit and I'd take off my agent hat and join in, but lately, I'd been feeling the pressure of my intense schedule. Maybe it was good timing having Willow come. Maybe I was overthinking things. Maybe everything was going to be totally fine and I needed to just lay off. After all, what could possibly be so horrible about spending time with my sister?

Chapter Two

The house was huge.

Intimidating.

It was three stories of financial security, determination, blood, sweat, tears—it was three stories of all the things I wanted out of my soccer career—out of my life.

I gulped at the sight of the modern house and its intimidating landscaping. My dad owned a landscaping business, so I knew the cost of a mature tree—or the cost of at least twenty with shrubs, flowers, intricate water fountains and a Japanese garden that looked so Zen I had the instinctual urge to let out the breath I was holding in and relax.

But I couldn't.

I was meeting one of the biggest sports agents in the world.

Matt Kingston.

Might as well call him King.

He was my best friend's older brother, and every single time she'd talked about him he'd sounded smooth, calculating, and damn good at his job. I didn't want to put all my eggs in one basket, but first impressions were everything. I got out of the rental car holding a plate of peanut-butter cookies in one hand and my backpack in the other, leaving the rest of my stuff behind. It was either this or move back in with my dad. The thought was daunting; we weren't close, at all. We saw each other during the holidays but other than that, I kept to myself. And after everything this last year, I needed a break. I needed . . . something.

"He's sweet! Bring him cookies!" We hadn't been in Seattle for even ten minutes before Willow hopped out of the car and instructed me to use her brother's sweet tooth against him. Stranded, I had no choice but to follow the directions to his mansion and hope for the best.

I exhaled and rang the doorbell, half expecting a butler to answer and ask me to take off my shoes before coming in or maybe mistake me for staff and tell me to enter through the back.

Note to self: this wasn't a historical romance novel.

This was my new life.

Hopefully, the start of a new career if I could get someone like Matt to negotiate on my behalf.

It was business.

Not personal.

I wasn't using my friendship.

I was just . . . networking.

Footsteps sounded on the other side of the door, and it jerked open so fast that I took a step back and almost dropped the plate of cookies. I shoved them forward. "These are for you."

As far as a first impression went, I could have done worse, right?

And then I locked eyes with him.

Not Matt.

I felt my body stiffen, my eyes widen. Jagger. I was staring at Jagger Komokov. One of the best goalies in the entire world.

He grinned. His long brown locks had been cropped, which is why I had thought he was Matt. "These for me?"

"Um . . ." What should I say? No? "Yes?" came out of my mouth.

"Matt!" Jagger yelled, not taking his eyes off me. "Girl Scouts are making the rounds . . ." I tore my gaze away and squeezed my eyes shut so I didn't further the stupid coming from my body or mouth.

"Girl Scouts?" a male voice yelled. "The hell! Get rid of them, we're in a meeting!"

Jagger shrugged, plate still in hand. "Sorry, but I think I'll keep these."

They were on a plastic plate.

With Saran Wrap.

They looked nothing like Girl Scout cookies, jackass.

I crossed my arms. "I'm here for Matt."

His eyebrows shot up. "Matt Kingston? That Matt? You sure?"

I ground my teeth. "Pretty sure."

"Sorry, I'm his new security, nobody gets past me."

I was killing Willow later. Give a girl some warning next time! Like, oh hey, there may be professional athletes just hanging out, try not to put your foot in your mouth like usual!

"You're not."

"Excuse me?"

"Security." I grinned. "You're Jagger Komokov, giant chip on your shoulder the size of the exact space some lucky bastard was able to get a ball into your net, what was it, from like seven feet?"

"Bullshit!" he roared.

I sidestepped him.

He moved.

I moved.

And then he took a cookie out from under the wrap and jammed it in his mouth. "Mmmm, peanut butter? You trying to kill him?"

"No!"

"What if he's allergic?" He grinned.

"His sister would have specified!" I was hot. Exhausted from our plane ride. And just needed to ask him where to put my bags! "Look, I'm tired. Can we do this whole weird interrogation later?"

I tried to get past him again.

He braced one hand against the door.

"Jagger! Stop eating all the fucking cookies and get your ass in here for damage control!"

"Told you Grandma was off her rocker!" Jagger called back over his shoulder and then whispered to me, "She called Matt a Russian spy when I got stopped for an interview outside a restaurant, it's all over the news. He shouldn't have worn red, and he sure as hell shouldn't have checked up on me, I got my shit handled." He shrugged and took another bite. "So, what will it be, little girl? You leave on your own or am I escorting you back to that . . ." He frowned. "Jetta."

"Nothing wrong with a Jetta." It was a cheap rental until . . . well, until my future happened.

"More of a sports-car kinda guy, you understand." He winked.

I was losing patience.

And my temper, which I'd been told was one of my worst qualities and just another one of the many reasons that some of the teams were leery of giving me a bigger contract. I was a risk they weren't sure they could afford to take!

"Move before I rip your balls from your body," I said with a smile and then swallowed and added, "Please."

He grinned. "Yeah, okay, small fry, go right ahead."

"Really?"

"No." He started closing the door. "Good cookies, though!"

The door clicked shut in my face.

I rang the bell a few more times.

And then I started aggressively pounding my hands against the solid wood.

It swung open.

"Listen, jackass—"

I almost swallowed my tongue as Matt Kingston stood to his full six-foot-four height and crossed his arms over a broad chest. A nice chest covered by a white button-down tucked into black trousers, and shiny shoes. He looked like he'd just had dinner with royalty.

His sleeves were rolled halfway up his forearms, and I could see golden muscle flex hard like he was clenching his fists in irritation. His light-blue eyes took inventory of me as if I wasn't worth him wasting any sort of words. His blond hair was mussed like he'd been running his hands through it.

He was beautiful up close. Equal parts masculine and serious. He had an air about him that both intimidated me and made me want to lean in closer.

"Speak," he rasped, jolting me out of my haze while I mentally applauded God for making such a fine specimen. Of course he couldn't be nice on top of being too handsome for words, because that wouldn't be fair to the female population, would it?

"I'm . . ." I gulped and then stood to my full height. "I'm Willow's friend."

"Good for you." He frowned. "Did you want me to pay you or something?"

"Pay me?"

"For her friendship. It's the only reason I can imagine you'd come all the way to my house and make such a vague statement. God knows the woman could test the fucking pope."

My lips twitched. "Uh no, don't need money. My name's Parker Speedman. Willow told me you said I could stay here. I just . . . I needed help with some of my bags, and my hands were full of cookies. She said the way to your heart was through your stomach."

He stared at me for at least five solid seconds before he slammed the door in my face and let out a string of curse words that I could clearly hear, which had me flinching, only to open it again like he hadn't just had a mental breakdown.

His smile was forced, his tone clipped. "Where are your bags?"

"Car." I gulped.

"Jagger!" he roared. "Bags!"

"The hell?" Jagger sauntered back toward us. "I'm the talent!"

"You're the pain in the ass and your grandmother got us on CNN with bad press. Get her damn bags, bring them to one of the guest rooms, and then you can go think about all the ways you can make it up to me."

He let out a laugh. "Come on, Matty, it wasn't that bad."

"That bad?" He shoved Jagger.

I took a step back. What kind of client-agent relationship was this?

"They did a body-cavity search!" Matt roared. "TWICE!"

Jagger bit down on his lower lip and then winked over at me. "He liked it, just won't admit."

"His hands were twice the size of yours. The FBI just had to take her seriously . . ." Matt shivered. "Just . . . get the bags, and I'll think about your punishment later."

"Kinky," Jagger drawled as he walked past me and toward my rental.

Matt was already on the phone when I turned back, his eyes blazing like he was ready to strangle anyone in his path. "Willow, lovely to talk to you. Any reason why I'm staring at an uninvited guest?"

Worst first impression goes to . . .

"I did not." He pinched the bridge of his nose. "Willow—" He glared at me. "Fine. Yeah. No. And stop laughing or you're sleeping outside." He hung up and stepped back as Jagger brought my bags through the doorway.

"Well?" Matt shrugged. "Are you coming or going?"

The wind picked up.

We locked eyes as I whispered, "Coming."

And I could have sworn something flickered in his gaze. His lips parted as the air between us charged.

"Alright then," he said softly and then left me alone in his foyer.

Chapter Three

Matt

"Speak," I barked once Willow sauntered into the house with at least three shopping bags as well as one blue Tiffany's bag dangling from her wrist.

Three. Hours. Later.

I stared. "New nails?"

"I went for an understated blush pink." She winked and then waved her fingers in my face. "You like?"

I lightly slapped her hand away, earning a pout. "What the hell were you thinking?"

She rolled her eyes and dropped the bags onto my new white leather couch. Her heels clicked against my industrial concrete floors. "I was thinking that I'm too good of a friend to let Parker live on the streets, especially when I promised her free rent for the next three months. It was either bring her with me to charm you to death or leave her homeless—"

I let out a growl.

She shrugged and flipped her hair. "Plus I did ask you, but you were just too busy with one of your football guys to pay attention."

"Soccer, he plays soccer." I wiped my face with my hands and wondered if jumping off the pier into ice-cold water would make any of this go away or just kill me swiftly. I eyed Willow. Handling her wasn't the issue, but handling her and one of her friends? One of her attractive friends with pretty eyes and a body I tried not to notice? Hell, I was going to lose my mind keeping them from the guys. "I manage athletes, big difference."

"Meh, is it, though?" She shrugged and grabbed a bottle of water from the fridge. "For what it's worth, I really like what you did with the place. It's modern yet warm. Is that a real fur rug?"

"No," I snapped then leaned my full body against the counter. "She's in the room across from the master." Which meant she was going to be sleeping a few feet away from me, fantastic.

"Okay?" Willow squinted at me like I was the slow learner. "Because?"

"Because I'm repainting the other six guest bedrooms and remodeling the master bathroom." Something I would have told her had I known that I was going to have an unannounced guest.

"Where am I sleeping?"

I had sudden visions of my sister outside on the patio with one blanket and a bottle of whiskey to keep her warm from the ocean breeze.

"You? Oh, outside. I bought a cot. You're welcome." I grinned smugly.

"Funny, aren't you?" She crossed her arms. "Seriously, where am I sleeping?"

"Mother-in-law suite above the pool house. I wasn't sure if you wanted to cohabitate this early into your lesbian relationship—big step and all." I shrugged.

She grabbed a pillow from the couch and chucked it at my face. I ducked just in time. "I'll have you know that if I did swing that way I probably couldn't get a better girlfriend. She's hilarious, extremely loyal, and did you see that girl's ass?"

I gulped.

No.

Because I'd basically sent her to her room within minutes of her arrival and was seconds away from using Jagger's body as a human shield to keep myself from staring at it. I'd always been a sucker for women with athletic bodies—calves, I was a calves man. I blamed the soccer, and she had calves I wanted to dig my fingers into. "No. I was too busy plotting your death, but I'll be sure to add looking it over to my to-do list for Tuesday."

"Still an ass." Willow smiled wide.

"And you're still a pain in my ass." I sighed. "So I guess we're even." I checked my watch. "Hope you can cook."

"Cook?" she repeated, eyes narrowing.

"Yeah, I have a meeting." She didn't need to know it was more like hanging out with friends who just so happened to be clients.

"Perfect!" She rubbed her hands together. "I'll come."

"The hell you will! You aren't an agent yet," I hissed. "Intern—say it with me—intern . . ." I drew it out slowly and then clapped it out for good measure just in case she was having trouble sounding out the really hard parts.

"You done?" she said in a bored tone.

"I'm never done. Not when it comes to you, sis."

"Hah!" She stuck out her tongue. "Are you meeting with athletes or friends?"

I rocked back on my heels. "I see what you're doing, it won't work."

"So, friends." She did a little dance. "I've got the perfect dress, who knew? What time?"

"You're a plague," I said in a defeated voice, staring down at my fake bear rug and wondering where I went wrong—oh right, I went wrong when I said yes. I was already under stress with the remodel. I'd put everything on hold because my plate was so full, nothing was near finished the way I wanted it, and my little sister was getting her way, like she always did. I didn't want to fight her because deep down, in the darkest crevice of my mind, I knew that I needed more help with the agency, I just had a hard time accepting her help when I knew the sort of people she would be working with on a daily basis. She needed a tough skin, and because I'd basically spoiled her for her entire life, I worried she might not have it. Add another roommate to the scenario and I felt trapped.

"Aw, Matty!" She fanned her face and then pressed a hand to her chest. "Why, bless your little heart!"

"Poisoning your coffee tomorrow, fair warning." I loved her too much, that was the problem.

She just shrugged. "Poisoned your coffee every day of high school—you're welcome for the tolerance."

I clenched my fists just as a door down the hall shut and feet shuffled across the concrete floor. Sneakers. She was wearing sneakers. My sister wouldn't be caught dead in sneakers. How were they friends?

Parker poked her head around the corner. She was wearing loose, low-slung jeans that looked like they had seen better days, a white crop top, and a pair of high tops with no shoelaces.

"You can't wear that." Willow shook her head. "Lucky for you I bought you a dress!"

"Dress," I repeated dumbly. "Will, for the last time, you aren't coming!"

"Oh." Heavy sigh. Full-on pout. Tear-filled eyes. "I guess we'll just . . . have a few guy friends over. I think I still have some X left after that last orgy. Maybe we'll even go to prison, I've always wanted to see the inside of one. Do you think I can be someone's bitch? I mean I'm already yours so . . ."

"Fuck." I tugged at my hair, then searched inside for any semblance of calm and came back empty. Parker looked from Willow to me like she wasn't sure if she should intervene or run.

"Matt, admit it, this is a really great opportunity to introduce me to some of your clients without the pressure of it being strictly business.

You can wine and dine them, introduce me, and then I can start getting to know them. Admit it, I'm right." She crossed her arms.

My eye twitched as I tried to conjure up a way to fight her logic. "Fine. You can come, no fangirling, no autographs, no crotch grabs or ass grabs, no phone number exchanges, Snapchats, Instagram photos. If you tag anyone in your live feed, I'll shut down every social media account you have." I inhaled then exhaled. "And no flirting. I don't care if that's just how you were made." I made air quotes. "It's unprofessional. Oh, Slade is married so you're going nowhere with that one, and Jagger's one bad choice away from being sent back to Russia." I sighed. "Just . . . be good."

"Good." Willow snorted. "This is my future. We'll be great! Right, Parker?"

Parker hadn't said one word the entire time, but her skin was pale and her lips were pressed together like she was afraid she was going to say something she'd regret. After a gulp, she nodded to me and then gave Willow a petrified look. What? Could they communicate without speech now? Plus, she seemed so calm next to Willow, almost shy. Maybe she was going to be easier than my own sister to deal with.

I probably owed both of them an apology.

But I was all out of fucks.

So I shrugged in Parker's direction and then stomped past both girls to get dressed with visions of whiskey dancing in my head.

Chapter Four

I tugged down my tight black dress so it covered my ass and shot Willow a murderous glare; this was the last time I ever said yes to any of her clothing choices. She knew I didn't wear dresses, just like she knew I wasn't the best at meeting new people. I had foot-in-mouth syndrome. I constantly said what was on my mind, and my therapist often told me that I lacked the emotional empathy to care if anyone around me was affected by my words.

I just . . . I didn't have time to babysit other people's feelings.

And right now, my sole focus was to break out after college, get signed to a team as fast as humanly possible, make enough money to find a stable place to live, and do what I love for as long as my body allowed me. I didn't just love the sport of soccer, I loved the way that it made me forget about everything bad in life. It was my focus, my reason for getting up in the morning. It was everything to me, and the fact that it could be taken away, or that I could end up working at Starbucks, terrified me. I wanted to go pro. Bad.

I gulped when Matt stopped walking and checked his watch. Willow was on his right, I was on his left. He looked at her, then whipped his head over to me. Was he waiting for me to say something? Why were we just standing outside the restaurant?

I cleared my throat.

He cleared his.

I tried not blinking.

He didn't back down.

"That's not a dress," was what he went with. Every word clipped with disdain like he had a right to tell me what I was allowed to wear. Who died and made him my father? It wasn't like he was that old. Willow said he was barely thirty!

"Pardon?" I snapped, then mentally berated myself for my harsh response. See? Foot-in-mouth was ready to strike again. I dug my fingernails into my palms and waited for his response.

"That"—he jerked his chin at me like I was a petulant child, and I ignored the butterflies that swarmed in my belly at his heated look— "is not a dress." He leaned in. "Dresses have fabric. They cover things that need to stay covered. That's a long tank top that should have been thrown out when you grew boobs in the eighth grade." He shook his head and paled, then mumbled awkwardly, "Not that I'm looking at your boobs."

I gritted my teeth as rage took over like it always did when I felt threatened or insulted. I pointed at the orange stripe resting on his chest. "Well, *that's* not a tie."

"Bullshit, this is a great tie!" Matt pulled on it a bit and stretched his neck. "It's marmalade and goes with my white suit."

"You look like a pumpkin-spice latte." I grinned. "But the really shitty kind they give away for free at the mall."

"Parker!" Willow hissed.

"What? He insulted my dress!" I argued, trying to hide the hurt I felt at his obvious dislike of me. Willow should have mentally prepared him for both of us as a package deal. I felt unwanted and annoying. Plus, I needed him, which just made the situation that much more dire. "And no rebuttal. Nice." I started to walk away only to have Matt grab me by the hand and jerk me back.

Willow cursed and pressed her fingertips to her forehead.

"Behave." His breath was hot on my ear. "I don't know you. In fact, I'm instantly regretting letting you into my house, but this night is important. These people may be friends, but they're still clients. Respect them or I'm finding you a nice cardboard box to call home in downtown Seattle. Got it?"

I sucked in a breath. "You would steal a box from people who are truly homeless?"

"What did I do to deserve this?" He looked toward the sky and then shook his head. "Let's go. Remember what I said." He paused and then added, "Both of you."

"Yes, Dad." I winked at Willow. My voice was shaky, and I felt the onslaught of tears. A few minutes in and I was already messing everything up! I focused on the embarrassment of him calling me out as anger clouded my line of vision. "We'll be good. Promise."

Regret came hard and fast as we made our way into the fancy, dimly lit restaurant.

What the hell was I doing?

I needed him.

And yet I had insulted his tie and called him names.

It didn't help that he was pretty to look at, with smooth, tanned skin, a white flashy smile, eyes that crinkled, and an expressive face that captivated me even though I didn't want it to. Yeah, and I'd called him Dad. Good one!

I took a calming breath. I could do this. I could be nice even if he was an ass. I just needed to keep my attitude in check.

How hard could it be?

Just because I've never particularly had that talent doesn't mean I can't suddenly develop it, over dinner, in a high-stress situation.

My smile felt brittle as we sat down at an elegant circular table. I recognized Jagger instantly, he winked at me and then looked ready to swallow his tongue when he locked eyes with Willow.

I watched the exchange with interest mainly because I wondered how Matt could have such a gorgeous little sister and not realize that every athlete that worked for him would probably do anything to get into her pants.

Huh.

Matt ordered a bottle of wine just as Slade Rodriguez walked in and sat across from us with a stunning woman on his arm. I'd read he'd gotten married.

I hadn't read that she was a supermodel.

Her smile was warm as she introduced herself to everyone.

Lastly was some guy from the Bellevue Bucks that I'm pretty sure could eat everyone at the table and still have calories to burn. He was gorgeous in a cocky way, and the woman on his arm had the most attractive curves I'd ever seen in my life.

As in, give-me-your-entire-workout-plan-so-I-can-find-my-ass sort of curves.

"So . . ." Slade gave Matt an amused look. "I heard you have new roommates."

Matt sighed and reached for the wine. "They can hear you. For the record."

"I know." A grin stretched across his face. "This pleases me more than it should." He nodded to Willow. "You still planning on following in his footsteps?"

She giggled. "You know it."

"Brave woman."

"And smart, don't forget smart." She pointed her wineglass at him as the table fell silent. All eyes moved to me.

Great.

Just don't yell.

Or insult anyone.

I forced a smile and waited while Slade's eyes narrowed and then widened in shock.

Oh no.

This was bad.

This was going to be very, very bad.

"Parker Speedman?" he said in a rich, deep voice.

"Uh, present?" I laughed lightly.

"Wow." He tossed his napkin down on the table. "Didn't you punch your own coach last year before the championship—"

"Yeah," I said quickly and reached for my wine, took two long gulps and then changed the subject. "So, Matt works for all of you?"

"Aw, I think I love this girl. She actually realizes we're the talent, not you." Jagger winked at Matt. "And yeah, we've been together a while, plus we make him money."

Matt snorted. "You're actually causing me to lose money when your racist grandmother tries to attack members of the media with a fork."

"Can't say I didn't warn ya, man!" Jagger laughed and shifted his focus to me. "So you punched your coach?" He leaned in. "What was that like? Invigorating? Powerful? What the hell was she doing that she deserved a punch?"

"He," I corrected, suddenly feeling sick to my stomach. "And we don't need to talk about it. Water under the bridge." Sweat broke out across my forehead as I tried to keep it cool on the surface while I was dying a little bit on the inside.

"Parker?" Matt said my name softly, but it was jarring, so I jumped in my seat and nearly spilled the water in my hand.

"Hmm, yes?"

"Are you okay?"

I swallowed and looked down at my lap. I tried to force a smile and look unperturbed. It had been a year of forced smiles and trying not to react, hadn't it? If this past year had taught me anything it was that all I had was myself, my dreams, and Willow. My dad had never wanted me to go pro, he put huge value on education and had always looked at soccer as a hobby. I swear he was relieved when my coach all but said he would blacklist me.

And that was the final nail in the coffin of my relationship with my dad.

Because I was his only daughter.

His flesh and blood.

And he never asked me why a coach would threaten his own athlete.

Never asked why I flinched when my coach touched my arm.

Maybe he knew.

Maybe he didn't want to know.

In my mind that made him just as bad as my coach, just as guilty.

"I'm fine." My voice sounded weak to my ears but I smiled at everyone around the table. I put on a show like I always did. I tried to make everyone believe I was great when inside I felt exactly the opposite.

I really needed to find a new therapist. One I could trust. One who didn't work for the college—one who didn't sleep with the very coach who sent me to see her in the first place.

"You look fine." Jagger frowned at me and then looked at Matt. "So, three months, huh? Nothing but estrogen floating around your house. You think your balls are going to shrivel up any smaller?"

"The real question is, can they get any smaller?" Slade piped up.

I smiled like everyone else.

And ate my food.

I nodded when people spoke to me.

I didn't cry when they talked about the game I loved so much.

It was like standing outside my body, watching the performance, coaching myself on all the right things to do so that I didn't mess up my last chance. It was emotionally and physically exhausting trying to keep that smile in place.

So when dinner was over, I slouched a bit in my chair before standing.

"Hey." Slade's wife, Mackenzie, put a hand on my shoulder. "You look like you're about to be sick."

I flinched. I hated being touched. Being touched reminded me of dark things done in dark places.

I politely stepped away from her as if she had startled me, and then shrugged. "It's just been a really long day."

She shook her head and tossed her caramel-colored hair. Her wide smile was so engaging it was hard not to smile back. "I have those often, so I get it. Well, I hope you stick around longer than the summer."

I sighed as my stomach dropped. "That all depends on if I get signed with a team."

"Signed?" Jagger butted into the conversation. "Who's interested?"

"As of right now, nobody," I said as Slade joined us, his penetrating gaze going right through me. I was ready to have a full-blown panic attack at the attention. It wasn't just that he was a big deal, he was a soccer god, his fan clubs had fan clubs, so the fact that he was even overhearing the conversation was sucking the oxygen from the atmosphere.

Mackenzie must have noticed because she rolled her eyes at the men as they waited for me to say more about my nonexistent career. "Could you guys give us a little privacy?"

Slade gave her a *What did I do* face before walking away.

She wrapped an arm around me, again causing me to tense up, and pulled me aside. "So you had interest and now no interest? I feel like there's more to the story, spill."

"I don't know you," I blurted stupidly. I didn't just blindly trust people, I'd learned that lesson the hard way. I'd barely even filled Willow in on everything. It gave me anxiety just thinking about it, and my chest tightened as I tried to suck in some air through my pursed lips.

"Which should make it easier." She stared at me.

I glared right back.

She didn't so much as flinch.

I decided I liked her. She reminded me of Willow. I liked strong women, and she seemed like one of those women.

Finally, I relaxed a fraction. "I have interest from Seattle." I didn't tell her that's where I really wanted to be, as far away from him as possible. "San Diego, LA, Florida, and a new team in Dallas."

Her eyebrows shot up. "Wow, that's quite a lot of offers."

"Interest. Not offers," I grumbled.

"No agent?" she guessed.

"Something like that." It was a partial truth. The whole truth could never come out. Ever. It would only destroy what was left of me.

"Hey, Matt!" Mackenzie actually called him over. I gave her a *What the hell* look. No, no, no! It wasn't supposed to happen like this! I was going to show him my stats, tapes of my playing, the normal thing! And if that wasn't enough to convince him to represent me I would go with plan B—baking cookies and getting him drunk off his ass! I wasn't supposed to ask for a favor three hours in! That's not how these things work! I felt my cheeks blush a bright red when she grinned at him. "You owe me a favor."

"So?"

"I'm calling it in."

"I don't recall this conversation."

"I think I was in the shower . . . with Slade." She tapped her chin. "Something about sexual harassment and—"

"What do you want?" he interrupted quickly.

She pointed at me with a triumphant grin. "Your new roommate needs an agent. Seattle's shown interest as well as other teams. Let the negotiations begin!" She nodded like it was just that easy.

Matt leveled me with a glare that had me ready to back into the dessert cart behind me. He didn't blink. His face didn't move. Every gorgeous angle of his face was taut with tension.

Great.

Thanks, Mackenzie!

"My rate is fifteen percent of whatever you earn."

I gulped and opened my mouth. He held up his hand.

"But since I don't know you, I'm going to take twenty-five percent of your first contract and we'll see where we go from there. What kind of offers were you given?"

"My coach wouldn't share that information with me," I whispered, trying to keep the sadness and anger out of my voice.

He rubbed his chin. "Maybe I should give him a call and—"

"No!" I blurted a little too loudly. "No, I mean . . ."

Everyone turned to look at me.

Shit.

I shouldn't have come.

I shouldn't have worn a tiny dress that fit Willow better than my thick thighs.

I squeezed my eyes shut and took a breath. "Can we please just leave him out of it? He's not a nice man."

Mackenzie elbowed Matt.

"Fine."

I exhaled in relief.

"I'll have Willow draw up a contract in the morning. You'll be her guinea pig, she'll assist me with you, and I'll try to make you"—he eyed me up and down—"look like a world-class athlete instead of a fifteen-year-old with a tiny dress on. How's that sound?"

"Like sexual harassment," I chirped.

Mackenzie burst out laughing. "I have a feeling this is going to be a great relationship!"

"My. Ass," Matt whispered under his breath and grabbed his keys. "Let's go, girls. Bedtime."

"Okay, Dad," Willow grumbled just as Matt jerked her away from Jagger's clutches. Jagger sent me a sultry wink as Matt opened our doors and put us in the Escalade.

He drove with his hands at ten and two the entire way home.

His face impossible to read.

His body? Tense.

I wondered if that tension had to do with me, his sister, or the fact that we were raining on his parade for the next three months and that I'd somehow just made it all worse.

Chapter Five

MATT

They hadn't even been in my house for twenty-four hours and already everything was changing.

I found a box of tampons in the hall bathroom.

Next to a can of aerosol spray that had a giant kangaroo on it and something about a twenty-four-hour hold.

For what? Your ponytail?

I broke out in a cold sweat when I spotted another toothbrush near the sink. It was red with sparkles. This bothered me. I had no idea why. It wasn't like it was the master bathroom. But it was still my fucking bathroom.

I narrowed my eyes as a hairbrush with exactly three dark hairs stuck in it sat alarmingly close to the toothbrush. She was a monster! A savage! Who put hair that close to something that goes inside your mouth? Just the thought had me shuddering as I turned off the light and closed the door behind me.

"Oomph!" Parker stumbled against me. I caught her by the biceps. And then was completely caught off guard that she actually had them.

Slightly firm in all the right places, yet completely soft.

Her brown eyes had speckles of gold near the center, and I imagined that on any given day they could change color depending on her mood. Her strong jawline made her look like a tomboy, but part of me wondered if it was because of the way she wore her hair. Tight ponytails and not a stitch of makeup. Like attracting someone of the opposite sex was the furthest thing from her mind.

She jerked away from me as though I was the offending party.

When she'd done nothing but insult me since she arrived at my house.

"Your hairbrush is scary close to your toothbrush, just thought you should . . . know." Fuck me, did I really just warn her about hair? What the hell was wrong with me?

I mentally slapped myself while she narrowed her eyes at me then back at the closed door. "You think you're going to be able to sleep tonight knowing how close together they are, or should you watch me move them farther apart? I don't want to cause any more gray hair." Her eyes moved to the side of my head like she was fixated on at least a million gray hairs shining in all their glory telling her that I was thirty going on thirty-one with no girlfriend and an empty future filled with lonely nights and a room full of rescue kittens.

"I don't have gray hair," I snapped.

Her eyes fell to the side of my head, and her eyebrows rose. "If you say so."

"What the hell is that supposed to mean?"

Parker let out a sigh that was cuter than it should have been. It also made her look less harsh, like she had a side that was all soft curves and laughter. "It means everyone gets old, you should embrace the gray."

"But—"

"I need to use the bathroom." She sidestepped me and put her hand on the doorknob. "But thanks for the warning. I'll be sure to manage my bathroom tools more effectively, especially since I know they'll be inspected every night before bed." With a sarcastic wink, she was inside and the door was shut in my face.

I gasped.

Raised my hand to knock again then turned on my heel. "What the hell?"

"You look lost." Willow laughed as she made her way down the hall in short shorts and a crop top that looked like it belonged to a toddler. Why was she back in the main house? I gave her space so I could still hold onto some of my manhood and dignity in my own home! So far it wasn't working, was it?

"Let me guess, these are your pajamas now?" I pointed at her and shook my head. "Thought we talked about this."

She sighed and hung her head then put her hands on my shoulders. "Matt, I appreciate the concern, but I'm a grown adult. Nobody is going to see me in these but me, m'kay? Plus, you really aren't my dad even though we both know you've been more of a dad than a brother."

My throat closed up as it always did when we talked about Dad. The usual anger boiled to the surface. I slammed it down and pulled her in for a hug. "I'm your older brother. It's my job to worry." Our parents had never truly been involved in our lives and had died when I was in high school and Willow was in junior high. They used money and gifts instead of hugs and words of affirmation. We were like little trophy kids you tell your friends about but don't manage to take care of. Willow and I only had each other. Sink or swim, we did it together. Always.

"Hah." She pinched my side and pulled back. "And as your younger sister and only sister, it's my job to worry about you too. You're thirty."

"Why does everyone keep reminding me of my age?" I wondered out loud, suddenly irritated with myself because it made me think of other things I didn't have yet. Success was easy. But I had nobody to share it with. It never bothered me before. I never thought twice about it.

Maybe it was because Slade had settled down, fallen in love with his other half, and a part of me wanted that sort of passion.

Or maybe I was just feeling sorry for myself because I had two college graduates putting their toothbrushes all over the place!

Yeah, I was going to go with that.

"Because," she said in a sweet voice as she gripped my hands and squeezed, "you should be settling down and getting married. I mean look at Slade."

I did a double take. Had I said any of that out loud?

"Man, look at you!" She slugged me in the shoulder. "You look like I just told you to take up synchronized swimming!"

"Do not," I argued.

"Your eyes bugged out of your head like you needed an oxygen mask. So yeah, good to know that fear of commitment is still strong in you."

I scowled. "It's not that. Trust me, you're not even close."

She nodded slowly and then took a seat on the couch, pulling a blanket over her lap. "I see, so when was your last serious relationship?"

I opened my mouth but she held out her hand to stop me.

"With a female who wasn't your client," she added with a knowing grin.

I swallowed and then shrugged. "I date some."

"Define 'some.'"

"I've gone on a few dates." Lame. How many dates that weren't business dates, though? Or networking dates? Or meetings?

I tugged at my shirt and licked my lips.

"Yeah, okay, I'm setting you up."

"The hell you will!" I roared.

"Do you want to die alone?" she countered.

"Seriously? You come into my house, eat my food, beg for me to give you a job, and after one day I'm suddenly dying alone?"

"At least you don't have cats . . . yet." She winked.

I just rolled my eyes. "Stay out of my love life, Willow."

"Or lack thereof!" She cackled as I paced in front of her, then I grabbed a throw pillow and flung it in her general direction as hard as I could.

"I'm happy." I spread my arms wide. "I party with celebrities and athletes on a daily basis. I get to summer in the Hamptons—"

She made a gagging motion.

I glared. "The right girl will come along. I'm just . . . patient, not because I'm lonely but because I'm happy."

"You're patient because you're . . . happy?" She narrowed her eyes just as Parker walked into the living room and took a seat next to her.

Surrounded by ovaries, wasn't I?

"He's happy?" Parker just had to ask in that snarky little voice with her hair—I gulped and did a double take.

Out. Of. The. Ponytail.

My eyes burned as I watched her sigh and then pull her hair around her neck and inspect it for what I could only assume was split ends.

Even that seemed sexy.

She had shots of caramel and red in her auburn hair, how had I not noticed that?

Or the thick, natural waves that fell past her breasts.

Shit, now I was noticing her breasts.

Does no one wear a bra anymore?

"No," Parker said drily. "Burned those during the parade, right, Willow?"

Must have said that out loud. I grimaced. "And to answer your question,"—I addressed her with a sternness that reminded me of my father and made me simultaneously want to strangle myself—"yes, I'm happy."

"Are you really happy if you have to convince others that you're happy?" She tilted her head, dropped her hair against her chest, and crossed her arms.

"Sleep." I shook my head. "I need to sleep. Try not to stay up too late."

Fuck. It was out before I could stop it.

Try not to stay up too late?

I hesitated, waiting for a rebuttal.

But both girls just shared a smile.

I glanced one last time at her hair, at her smile, at the easy way she talked with Willow like she didn't need a wall to protect her.

And then I shook my head as I walked back toward the master bedroom and stared at myself in the mirror.

I was happy.

Wasn't I?

I had everything a man could want.

Everything.

Then why did I feel defeated?

Chapter Six

I was so nervous I couldn't sleep.

He said Willow would draw up my contract in the morning. My contract. Between Matt Kingston and me.

Matt. Kingston.

The same Matt Kingston whose eyes I couldn't look away from last night. The guy who oozed sexuality like it was an extension of his expensive cologne. The guy that I caught staring at me with such heat I pretended to be staring at the tips of my hair. Since when have I ever cared about my hair?

He was rude.

Often irritated, if I was to judge him based on the last twenty-four hours.

But he was also something else.

Really damn good-looking.

And rich.

And successful.

And one of the best agents, if not the best, in the sports world.

I squeezed my eyes shut as my heart thudded against my chest. I had to be up in a half hour if I was going to get a run in before breakfast.

Willow usually slept in until nine.

I wasn't sure what Matt's schedule was, and I berated myself when I realized I wanted to know if he got up early and worked out. If he still missed the game, hungered for it in the way I would every day of my life if I didn't get signed to a team.

And fast.

I groaned into my pillow and hit my hands against the mattress.

Too many uncertainties.

Yet another man who held my future in his hands.

Focus.

What was I good at?

Running plays, loving the game with all my heart, and getting into fights when people got in my way.

Well, that and attracting all the wrong sorts of attention.

How the hell was I supposed to get on a team when I couldn't even manage to make it through a dinner without wanting to either lash out or pass out on the spot from an anxiety attack?

I threw the covers off, grabbed my Nikes and some running shorts, and pulled on a baby-blue sports bra. My AirPods were waiting on the nightstand, and my phone was already in my hand ready to go when I started the music.

I sucked in a breath through my nose, exhaled, and then nodded my head to the beat as my feet took me out of the guest room, down the hall, and out the door.

Just me and the road.

Freedom.

My feet pounded the pavement as my breathing quickened. This was what I needed, an escape, a bit of suffering to remind myself why I was putting myself at Matt's mercy.

I focused on the job.

On my game.

On my breathing.

On everything but the fact that his eyes haunted me with each step, just like his smug smirk over dinner and his disdain at being forced to work with me.

I stopped and shook my head as Post Malone's latest pounded in my eardrums.

It didn't matter.

None of it did.

Because I wouldn't quit.

Ever.

I was going to make it.

Or die trying.

I kept running with a smile on my face.

Make the world your oyster.

And if that doesn't work?

Make it your bitch.

An hour later, I stumbled into the house, sweaty and ready to eat anything and everything including the first human who spoke to me. My stomach grumbled as I pulled out my pods and set them on the counter along with my phone. Frowning, I glanced around the dark house.

Did Matt sleep in?

Was he a night owl?

My jaw clenched.

Did it matter what he did with his time?

I gave my head a shake and made my way toward the bathroom. I was in the process of peeling off my sweaty bra just as I pushed open the door and looked in the shower.

The shower that was on.

In the bathroom that was occupied.

Please let it be Willow. Please let it be Willow.

Why the heck wasn't the door locked?

Slowly, I backed away and was halfway out the door when the shower door opened and out stepped Matt in all his naked, tanned glory.

I took another step backward.

"Morning, Parker!" Willow chirped, making her way down the hall with a cup of coffee in hand as she headed back out to the pool house, oblivious to my red face and the fact that I was halfway in the bathroom with her naked and, by the looks of it, pissed-off brother.

I gulped. "Sorry, I didn't—the door wasn't locked, and I was—"

Matt's eyes heated.

And that's when I realized I was holding my bra in my hands.

I was topless.

A good way, some might say the best way, to start a business relationship. Hah. I winced and then tried covering my breasts with the black scraps, only to do it upside down and just show him more nipple.

His jaw clenched.

I stepped back. "Really, just . . . really sorry."

At least his towel had made it around his hips.

"Shut the door," he said through clenched teeth.

"Yup!" I moved back and slammed it closed and stared at it a few seconds while my breathing evened.

Something hit a wall. I exhaled roughly and tiptoed back into my room, then waited in a weird tense silence for footsteps down the hall. He passed my room without looking in.

I hated that it bothered me.

That after seeing nipple he wouldn't even really acknowledge that said nipples belonged to me.

Why did it even matter?

I grabbed my things and dashed back into the bathroom. I turned the shower on just in time to peel my sweaty shorts down and bare my ass toward the very door that then swung open, revealing Matt.

He just stood there.

My heart slammed against my ribs. *No . . . it's not like before.*

"What are you doing!" I yelled when I found my words. A navy-blue bath towel hung from the rack a few feet away. I glanced at it but forced myself to meet his gaze, to keep his eyes locked on mine. *Not the same, not the same. Don't back down. Never back down again.*

He held up one finger, two fingers, three, and then he tilted his head and grinned smugly. "The amount of seconds you stared before shutting the door. Feels invasive, right?"

"It wasn't locked!" I said for the second time, my voice wavering.

He rolled his eyes. "It doesn't lock."

"Why are you still standing there?" Unable to stop myself, I snatched the towel and covered myself.

He grinned. "Tit for tat."

"Leave!" I ground out.

"Leaving." And then he turned one last time. "Walk in on me again, and I'm brushing my teeth while you pee, got it?"

Anger rose, threatened to take over the situation, but I pushed it back with sarcasm. "Wow, living dangerously now, hmm?" My hairbrush was on the floor next to the wall. Ah, that was the object he threw. "Oh, and I'll be sure to put my brush away next time."

"See? All I ask for is a bit of compromise," he said before slamming the door so hard it caused one of the picture frames above the toilet to fall to the floor.

I gave two middle-finger salutes to the door and then jumped in the shower. It wasn't lost on me that my skin was flushed.

It also wasn't lost on me that the hot water had nothing to do with it.

Because the bastard had used it all!

"Matt!" I roared as my teeth chattered. It was going to be impossible to rinse the shampoo out of my hair. "Bastard!" I cursed him to hell and could have sworn I heard laughter down the hallway.

Chapter Seven

Matt

Everywhere I looked I saw nipples.

Skin.

A lot of skin.

Ass cheeks.

More skin.

I slammed my orange juice down onto the counter and wheeled around when I heard Willow and Parker make their way into the kitchen.

"You!" I pointed at Parker. "If you want to work with me, could you please stop walking in on me while I shower?"

"You," she countered, hands on hips, "could have been a gentleman and not used all the hot water or walked in on me to make a point!"

Willow gave me a confused look. "I miss all the good stuff by being stuck in the pool house!"

Parker's chest heaved, she crossed her arms over breasts I would never forget—ever—while I seethed and looked in the other direction. "Let's get one thing straight. I'm going to be your agent, not your friend, not your boyfriend, not the guy you lived with for three months. Agent." I said it slowly so she'd get the picture. "This means you walk around with clothes on. This means you don't peel off said clothes before you reach the bathroom. It means we have a professional line we don't ever cross. Ever." I gulped as my brain repeated a few more *evers* for good measure then flashed me an image of her tits again.

Shit.

I flinched at the need to rub my eyes to see if it would do the trick, as if I could just rub the nipples away.

"I don't date older men," she said in a low, semiaggressive tone that had my dick twitching behind my fly like it was excited at the thought of getting attacked by the person the voice belonged to.

"The hell?" I craned my neck at her. "Did you just call me old? Again? In my own house?"

"Sore spot," Willow coughed and then pounded her chest.

"We aren't doing whatever this is, where you can't help but have the last word, bait me, then make both of us look like asses."

"Both?" Parker said, questions lingering behind her eyes. "We sure about this *both* thing?"

My jaw clenched.

"His neck vein is throbbing," Willow said in a hushed whisper as she drummed her fingernails across the granite counter. "I would tread carefully."

Parker's eyes widened before she gave me a barely noticeable nod. "Sorry, I get it. We'll keep it professional. I can do it. Whatever you need me to do, I can do."

She just had to lick her damn lips, didn't she?

And they just had to look plump, swollen.

More visions of her naked flitted across my brain.

This was going to be the hardest three months of my life in more ways than one.

"Great." I clasped my hands together. "Now that we have that all out of the way, I'm going to make some calls to a few different teams, send out some feelers. In the meantime, I want Willow to sell the shit out of you. Tell her your stats, awards, accomplishments. I want everything. If you saved a kitten from a fire when you were six, I need to know about it. Won a spelling bee when you were eight. Hell, if you played multiple sports and got something more than a participation trophy, I need it. I'll also need your transcripts from college, background information, family information, and we'll need to do a full physical."

She paled.

"Parker?" I snapped my fingers in front of her. "You got all that?"

She nodded slowly. "Yes, I just . . . yes. I don't like . . ." She looked down at her feet; but right before she did I caught something like vulnerability and maybe even a flash of pain in her eyes. "Can I please just request a female doctor?"

I made an annoyed sound. I wouldn't let a male doctor near her, not after all of the shit going down in the sports world surrounding male doctors treating female athletes. "Absolutely."

She exhaled. "Okay, good, thank you. That would be . . . thank you."

Willow gave her a curious look.

I felt like I was missing something until Parker grinned over at Willow and said, "Remember Dr. Lee from sophomore year?"

Willow pressed a hand to her heart. "So gorgeous! I swear I tried to sprain my ankle on a daily basis just so he would say in that accent of his, 'You're benched!'"

"I would have gone to his bench any day." Parker laughed.

"You were too good a player." Willow winked. "Even with a sprained ankle."

"As much as I love this journey down memory lane," I said as I grabbed my cell from the counter, "I'm going to be in my office working."

Willow pouted. "Do I get an office?"

"Intern." I grinned. "Say it with me, inter—"

She grabbed a pillow and waved it high in the air like she was going to chuck it at my face or maybe even try for my balls.

I smirked. "You can work in the living room or theater room. It's nice. You can even set up camp outside, grab your laptop, and get to work. No more talking about the past. We need to focus on Parker's future. And, Willow? That's your job. Don't fail her. I don't have to remind you that representing friends and family never ends well, which means you've got your job cut out for you."

"Good thing we aren't friends," Parker piped up, her venom directed at me. And all I could conjure up was an image of us being anything but friendly in the shower.

And me pulling her hair.

Running my hands over—

I locked eyes with her and whispered gruffly, "Good thing."

Chapter Eight

PARKER

I nervously tucked my feet under my body while Willow's fingers flew across the keyboard. For some reason the tap, tap, tap of her nails had me cringing the longer we sat there.

It had been a painful three hours.

Three hours where I did nothing but talk about myself while Willow did the appropriate *uh-huhs* and then the tap, tap, tap.

I dug my hands into the throw pillow, ready to toss it across the room.

I wasn't meant to be indoors.

Sitting.

My legs itched to run.

My body pulsed with the need to just be outside and do something active. Nervous energy pounded through me until it was so hard to concentrate that I wanted to scream.

"Okay, let's talk about this last year." Willow sighed. "I think I have most of the information I need, since we were practically sleeping in the same bed every night."

I gave her an annoyed look. "You said you'd replace your bed then kept forgetting. You're lucky it wasn't a twin."

"It was more comfortable than mine would have been."

I sighed. "Admit it, you're afraid of the dark."

She just grinned at her screen. "I admit nothing. Okay, so this last season you won MVP then had the title stripped after . . ." She cleared her throat like she wasn't sure what else to say.

And she'd be right about that.

After I punched my coach.

After I ruined my life.

After I said no.

I hugged my chest and shook my head at the ground like it held all the answers along with all the memories of him, the moments leading up to life-changing circumstances that should have made me a hero instead of a villain.

"Can we take a break?" I croaked, already standing and tugging my ponytail out and messing up my hair. My head ached from stress, not the tight ponytail, but my heart and my suddenly nauseated stomach were having none of it.

"Sure!" she chirped, jumping to her feet and slamming the laptop closed. Her loose hair fell in waves around her bronze shoulders and a shot of envy ran through my body at how easy she always seemed to make things . . . as if the world was at her feet. When for the last few years, it had deemed me unworthy and decided to sit on my face instead.

My eyes flickered to the sliding glass door that overlooked the gorgeous view of the Sound. The water looked so peaceful I actually felt better; then again, if I had a multimillion-dollar view to look at every day, I imagined I'd feel a lot less anxiety. With a smile tugging at my lips, I realized that it had been forever since I'd taken the time to focus on and appreciate the beauty around me. I'd been so hell-bent on hiding that it never occurred to me to stop and take a deep breath. Lately everything had felt like an uphill battle, like the world was against me—until now.

I opened the door and walked out, leaning my forearms on the wood railing just as I heard the sound of cursing followed by a door opening.

I jumped back when Matt stomped out of his office a floor just above and to the right, its balcony overlooking the same spot just a few feet away. I could probably make the jump if I tried. I was about to say hi when he started yelling again.

"No shit." He ran a hand through his perfectly mussed hair and then looked up at the sky, squinting his eyes. "I know, I know, that's just not what I wanted to hear, Darius."

He adjusted his Bluetooth headset.

Mouth dry, I watched him stretch his arms over his head, giving me a perfect view up his shirt of his lower abs. Damn, the man was cut.

I shook the thought from my head.

Sexy bodies didn't always equal good hearts. I found that out the hard way. Just because the package is wrapped up in tight muscles that make your mouth go dry does not mean that there isn't ugly beneath the surface.

Or something terrifying.

In fact, it almost made me more nauseated to think about it. To think about how easy it was to fall for someone's camera-ready looks, white teeth, bronzed skin, and perfect smile.

So damn easy to fall in love with a public persona not realizing that behind closed doors they were a different person entirely. Plus . . . guys his age—not that he was ready to sign up for the early-bird special—typically wanted more than a girl who was all about sports, all about focus and drive.

They wanted a wife.

Not a co-captain.

A girlfriend who could take care of them.

Not an athlete who would rather wear cleats to dinner and hated the idea of anything pink.

"Darius." Matt's tone changed. "All I'm saying is you owe me a favor, and because nobody else will even touch this girl—" He sighed. "Look, I'm desperate. I have to get her another interview and tryout with at least one club." Matt leaned against the railing. "She's not that bad." His face said I *was* actually that bad, and for some reason it hurt more than it should.

I felt myself start to become smaller, the way some people do when they don't want to be noticed, and I hated it. I hated it so much. That was part of what made me angry and always ready to lash out.

Because I had never been that girl before last year.

I once believed I was born to be brave and free.

I once believed I was born of fire.

And all it took was one person to steal that fire and leave me with nothing but ash.

I drew in a deep breath and decided to let him have his privacy. I knew I couldn't take it personally. To a lot of people I was that emotionally unhinged girl who attacked her coach on national TV, not exactly what you want on your team.

I wasn't sure what I was thinking in coming here.

That he'd be able to perform a miracle?

Defeat slammed down so hard that my shoulders ached.

"The stats prove it. Let me just work on the rest of the package." Matt's voice hit me just as I touched the sliding glass door. His laughter sounded a bit cruel. "I know, I know, but we can't all be my sister, alright?"

I flinched.

"She just needs a little bit of polishing." Another laugh. "Yeah, maybe some anger management, or at least a tip on how to bring in sponsorships that don't reference dog food, am I right?"

He laughed harder.

Anger and sadness fought each other as I clutched the door handle, unable to let go as his voice floated over the pounding of my pissed-off heart.

"Thanks, Darius. Tell the wife I said hello!" Another hard laugh. "No, no, I promise she'll be every bit as good as the hype." When he hung up, I didn't miss the way he uttered, "At least I hope."

I squeezed my eyes shut. I couldn't look at him and couldn't trust myself not to either cry or jump to his balcony and hold his body over the edge with a cruel smile on my face, all the while asking him what animal I looked like in that moment before I ripped his pretty smile off.

Maybe that was a little harsh.

Maybe the anger-management comment wasn't far from the mark.

"What team?" I finally found my voice.

"Damn it!" He didn't hide his irritation. I heard stomping, didn't see it, my eyes still closed and all that. "What the hell are you doing outside my office?"

"I was outside the living room, big difference, and I was taking in some fresh air." I finally turned and opened my eyes. "What team?"

"How much did you hear?" His eyes flickered from the door to my face. I couldn't get a read on anything except that his posture was tense and his face looked anything but apologetic from the strong line of his jaw to the eyes that seemed to look past my soul toward something darker, something locked up forever.

He was the sort of man that wanted to see a person's heart, understand how it worked, and ask you to trust him.

But he wasn't the sort of man a woman trusted.

He was just like everyone else.

A chameleon.

He was who he needed to be when he needed to be it.

And in that moment, I hated him more than I should.

"What. Team?" I finally hissed out a third time.

"Seattle Reign." He grinned like I should be happy, when all I felt was despair that the one team I'd really wanted needed to be bribed. "Wow, no 'Thank you, Matt'? 'You're the best agent in the world because you got me a tryout with the Reign'? Everyone's first choice right now? What an incredible opportunity to not fuck something up."

"He owed you a favor," I said lamely, voice hoarse. Was I really that bad?

"Doesn't matter," he clipped harshly. "What matters is—" He frowned. "What matters is you need to stop wearing your ponytails so tight, it makes you look angry all the time, and if you don't stop scowling at me I'm going to force Willow to go show you a true Botox experience."

"Why use her when I could just ask you?" I answered sweetly.

He glared. "Everything you see is real, Cheetah Girl."

I gawked. "Who told you?"

"Willow did a very extensive report, at least the early report she sent before I got on that last phone call was"—he smirked—"enlightening."

Heat rushed into my cheeks while my brain basically screamed, *Upper hand, get it back, fast! He's your opponent, don't give him the damn ball! Steal it back!*

But I had nothing except, "At least I was good enough to get a nickname."

He stopped smiling immediately. "Low blow for someone who holds your future in his hands, don't you think?"

"I've heard that before." It was out before I could stop myself.

Confusion marred his face. "What do you mean?"

"Nothing." I cleared my throat. Just then, I was saved by the doorbell. "I got it!"

Thankfully, the sliding glass door was already open. Otherwise, I would have face-planted right in front of Matt, and every bird in the vicinity would have had a good laugh.

Willow was already opening the door.

And in walked Jagger with his swagger. I couldn't help but grin as he winked at me and then reached for Willow's hand and kissed the back of it. "Damn, you're pretty."

I made a gagging noise just in time for Matt to walk in with thunder in his steps and murder in his eyes. "Just tell me you aren't going to prison with your grandma, and I'll forget the fact that you just kissed my sister's hand!"

"Not joining Grandma, but I can hold out hope." He laughed. "I was just in the neighborhood, so . . ."

Matt looked at Jagger then at me, then back at Jagger. "Too bad you're leaving the neighborhood. You got your gear at the stadium?"

Jagger gave Willow an apologetic look when Matt turned around to grab a water. "Sure do."

"Road trip." He nodded to me. "Get your shit, Cheetah Girl, practice starts this afternoon."

"Wait." I held up my hand. "Practice? What do you mean practice?"

"I mean"—Matt was already walking down the hall and yelling over his shoulder—"that you have to impress the team at your tryout, and the only way you're going to do it is if you have the best in the world training you."

Made sense. "So, Jagger's just going to train me out of the joy of his very Russian heart?"

Jagger put his hand over his chest and nodded solemnly.

"Nope!"

"What?" We said in unison, Willow included.

"I said the best." Matt stopped and didn't turn around. "Which means I'm training you while you kick as many balls as you can at Jagger's face."

I snorted out a laugh while Jagger glared. "Bring your cup."

He eyed me up and down. "Think I'll wear two."

"Good man." Willow elbowed him a bit while Matt disappeared around the corner.

I was too focused on Willow and Jagger, all of a sudden whispering under their breath, to realize it too late.

Until I heard cleats on the slate floor.

Until I felt a sickness rush over my body.

Matt, older Matt, didn't just become my agent.

He was in joggers and a white vintage shirt with some sort of soccer graphic on the front.

No. Because an agent I could handle.

An agent meant that it was all business.

But he'd just made it personal . . .

By stepping into a position of a mentor, someone I would need to respect, to look up to in order to learn from.

And history suddenly felt very much like it was repeating itself as he tied his cleats and looked at me with a dangerous amount of heat that shot straight through my body.

"What?" He jerked his head up at me and smirked. "Intimidated?"

"Yeah," I croaked then swallowed back my emotions. "Something like that." I tucked my hair behind my ears as the sting of tears made itself known. "Let me just go grab my gear."

He stood and crossed his arms. "You have three minutes."

He didn't see my tear-stained cheeks. I wiped them as soon as the tears fell, catching a few between my fingertips before they even touched my skin.

He didn't see my bloodshot eyes. I grabbed sunglasses for that.

And he didn't see the way my heart shook in my chest at the thought of training one-on-one.

With another man.

An older man.

An experienced man.

A man not used to the word no.

Chapter Nine

MATT

I wasn't sure what possessed me to offer to train Parker other than my severe lack of tact when it came to the conversation she overheard. Why the hell should I feel guilty for doing my job? And for saying or doing anything to get her what she wanted while at the same time getting what I wanted, which was her and my sister out of my space?

She'd been there two days and she was everywhere.

Taking over everything.

The most annoying thing being all the rational space in my head.

Off-limits.

In every way.

Not to mention she tended to apparently hate the male race, if what I read in every newspaper report was accurate, not to mention the reports from two of the other team captains and the coach himself.

He sounded like an arrogant piece of work.

But every single female on that team looked at him like a soccer god. He was a good-looking European dumbass who I remembered playing maybe once or twice before we both left the league for our own reasons.

Mine was my injury and inability to come back from it, even with the right drugs.

And his?

At this point it looked like the general consensus of his teammates was that he was a selfish asshole who wanted all the glory in a team sport that needed every single player for every single goal.

I had no space for assholes in my life.

I already had my clients.

And between Jagger and Slade I had my hands full. Then again they were getting along a lot better since Slade was getting laid on a regular basis and had a wife who put up with him.

Jagger on the other hand made me want to sleep with whiskey under my pillow and a Xanax clutched in my left hand just in case.

I banged on the women's locker-room door one more time. "Parker, you don't even wear makeup, putting on shorts takes thirty seconds max, and that's if you keep getting confused between your right and left leg because your dick's in the way and you don't have a dick—"

Jagger elbowed me.

"*What?*" I mouthed, and he shook his head. "So hurry the hell up. Just because you're a woman doesn't mean—"

The locker-room door jerked open, making me stumble back a bit. "Ready."

She was wearing a long-sleeved black shirt and matching shorts.

The shorts I understood.

The long-sleeved shirt confused me. She was going to get hot, sweaty.

I frowned then wiped the mental image of a hot and sweaty Parker from my consciousness.

She just shoved past us like we were the ones taking years to get ready in the locker room.

"Face looks puffy," Jagger said under his breath.

"What? Mine?" I wiped my face.

He rolled his eyes. "You can be a dick sometimes. You get that, right?"

"I'm a dick so you don't have to be, and yet here we are." I spread my arms wide. "You should pay me more."

"You make more than most athletes, and last week one of the Toms called you to go jet-setting to Brazil. I think you're going to make it." He chuckled.

I grinned. "God, I love my job . . . you know, when your grandmother isn't using racial slurs."

"She's a real treat, my grandma. Don't say I didn't warn you."

I sighed as we walked into the stadium. "Yeah, well, I thought you were being sarcastic, since that's you on a normal day."

Jagger stared after Parker. "Something doesn't add up, and why are her cheeks puffy?"

"Stop staring at her cheeks, man, it's weird." I elbowed him and heaved a bag of balls over one shoulder. "She's a girl, they cry; just ask my sister about Jon Snow, and you'll be consoling her for the next hour."

"But Jon Snow didn't die," Jagger pointed out quietly.

"HE DIDN'T DIE?" Parker yelled across the field. "I HAVEN'T GOTTEN TO THE NEXT SEASON YET, YOU ASSHOLE!"

And then she was charging toward us at full speed.

"Think I know why she punched her coach." Jagger dropped his bag of balls and started running in the other direction. "Good luck!"

"Traitor!"

He just kept running. The bastard was probably going to go do his own workout and leave me to my own devices. Typical Jagger.

When she finally made it to me, I held up my hand for her to stop.

And when she didn't stop, I grabbed my fucking whistle and blew it.

Her chest heaved as she stopped inches from my body. "You don't just shout spoilers like that!"

"He wasn't shouting!"

"I have superhuman hearing when it comes to *Game of Thrones*, it's my spiritual gift." She grinned.

I sucked in a breath.

I was completely thrown off by her easy smile and the way it charmed itself into my soul so effortlessly. It made me want to smile back and laugh, and ask her to do it some more, just in my general direction.

Coach.

Agent.

I cleared my throat. "Jagger said your cheeks are puffy."

She touched her cheeks, which just brought my attention to how plump and delicate they were on an otherwise constantly pissed-off face. She was pretty when she smiled, but she didn't do it often enough.

And it made me wonder too much.

It made me want to dig when I had no business digging.

Coach.

Agent.

"Are you still wanting all of this?" I spread my arms wide as the stadium lights lit above us, the smell of turf filled the air, the empty stands awaited the crowds that would fill them screaming her name.

No better high.

No better drug.

Her eyes lit up. "Yeah, I'm fine, just allergies. And yes, I want this, I want all of this."

I hesitated then lowered my voice, picked up one of the balls, and tossed it to her. "Prove it." She licked her lower lip, which I found entirely too distracting, so I looked away. "Prove it and I'll get you everything."

"That's a mighty big promise, Matt Kingston."

I grinned at the way she said my name, like I was the biggest asshole on the planet. Why did I like it so much, then? Especially since I tried to be easygoing, at least with my male athletes. She had no respect for authority, though, so asshole it was.

"Alright." I jerked my chin toward the field. "Show me why they call you Cheetah Girl . . ."

She jogged off, laughing. "Think you can handle me?"

The air charged, and my eyes stupidly flicked to her ass as she ran off. And while I wanted to smugly say yes, part of me was already shaking my head no.

And I had no idea why except she wasn't what I expected in any way, and it threw me off that I couldn't manage her the way I would someone else. I sacrificed for my clients and they expected it.

That's how it worked.

I gave them the world—but first, they had to let me into theirs.

And I had a distinct feeling that Parker would never let that happen.

Not that I ever walked away from a challenge.

She stopped midfield.

I chased after her and kicked the ball between her legs. "Alright, Cheetah, impress me with your speed."

"Oh, that's not why they called me Cheetah Girl," she said softly before she ran around me, kicked the ball between my legs, and dribbled around my body like I was a toddler in training. She then kicked the ball toward the goal, hitting it directly down the middle with a perfect strike.

Still confused, I waited, and then she started doing a little dance. "Get it? Cheetah Girl? I was a sucker for Disney."

My jaw dropped. "Wait, so they called you Cheetah Girl because of the group?"

"And the fact that I would sing their songs to get myself hyped and do a little choreographed dance after . . . I'm Disney through and through, baby."

Yeah, right. I pointed toward the goal. "Do that again."

She did.

I grinned. "Again."

She groaned.

And when I asked her a tenth time she was past groaning and ready to murder me, especially when I said, "Your legs lost some strength since the last tape I reviewed . . ."

"So—"

"Lunge the field."

"The entire field?" she roared.

"With a ball in each hand." I pulled out my whistle and blew it in her face.

Three hours and exactly thirty-two minutes later.

"Again." My smile was wide while she wiped her face with the bottom of her shirt. She was dripping in sweat; steam was coming off her body as she ran through the cones dribbling the ball and then stopped to do ten burpees on each side of the cones before running through them and ending with jumping jacks and mountain climbers.

"You," she heaved as she did her jumping jacks, "are Satan!"

"Make sure to breathe with your diaphragm, expand in and out, not in shallow breaths," I instructed, tossing my whistle in the air and catching it.

She dropped to her hands and toes for mountain climbers, glaring at me as sweat dripped off her chin. "Is this really necessary?"

"Did you just growl at me?"

"Did you just yawn!"

I grinned so hard my face hurt. "Sorry, I was bored. You weren't going fast enough."

That earned me a middle finger.

"You know we should really work on that angry streak."

More middle fingers.

I let out a sigh. "Parker, coaches want someone they can mold, someone who listens to authority, and as a player you want to be someone that can sponsor something—"

"Other than dog food." She rose to her feet, chest heaving. "Yeah, got that part this morning, thanks for the vote of confidence."

"Does it help that it would be designer dog food for angry, crusty dogs who just need love?"

Silence.

"I'll take that as a no. Look, you want good endorsement deals."

"So you get paid more?" She crossed her arms and then shook out her hands and said something under her breath before peeling her shirt over her head and revealing a black sports bra top that kissed her belly button.

Causing my every thought to go south and get dirty real fast.

Coach.

Agent.

Her eyes darted away from me with uncertainty. Her body was lean, toned. I'd seen it earlier, obviously, but something about us being alone made it a thousand times more tense than when we'd been at my house where Willow could walk down the hall at any minute.

I cleared my throat. "Not so I can get paid more, so that you can get paid more and so that you get bigger and better deals. I have money. No offense, but I don't need you for more of it."

"So now I'm charity?" She put her hands on her hips.

"Enough talking." I blew my whistle.

"Seriously!" she roared. "What now! We've been here for at least three hours."

I checked my watch mainly to keep myself from looking at her chest as it continued to heave in my direction with sweat dripping between her breasts. "Yeah, you're right, I'm starving."

"Oh, thank God!" She started jogging toward me.

I pulled off my whistle and made my way to the locker rooms, and she followed close behind. I waited until her hand was on the locker-room door then cleared my throat.

She hung her head. "What? What now? What could you possibly do to me at this point that would exhaust me any more?"

Her eyes widened a bit while I tried to think about anything but the fact that we were alone.

And she was beautiful.

Sweaty and beautiful.

More beautiful than when she was dressed up in a tight short dress.

More beautiful than any woman that sweaty had a right to be.

Shit.

I forced a cruel smile I wasn't feeling. I forced myself to replace the lust with cruelty, and I hated myself for it. "You're jogging home."

"That's at least five miles!" she bellowed.

"Six and a half, actually." I shrugged. "I'll grab your bag, though."

"No!" She held up her hands as every inch of color fell from her face, even her lips turned a grayish white. "No, um, I'll just leave it here and pick it up later."

"Don't be ridiculous." I rolled my eyes. "I'll just—"

"No!" She shoved against my chest this time.

I wasn't a violent man, or even really aggressive, but the fact that she just shoved me like I was about to attack her pissed me off. "What the hell is wrong with you?"

"Me?" Was it my imagination or was she shaking? "You're the one who wants to go into the girls' locker room alone and grab my . . . bag." It's like as she said it she realized how crazy she sounded, or maybe she was just embarrassed. "Never mind, I'll see you at home."

She shoved away from me and ran down the hall fast enough for me to stare after her in utter confusion.

I gave my head a shake and pushed the locker-room door open and went in search of her bag.

It was black.

Shocker.

I walked over to grab it and tripped over a cleat that I didn't see, sending the bag sailing to the floor. A few things spilled out.

Advil.

A water bottle.

And lastly, a prescription pill bottle with the label rubbed off.

And suddenly everything made sense.

Her anger.

Her irritation.

The way she was easily set off by anything or anyone.

Disappointment hit me so hard I had to sit. I shoved everything back into her bag as quickly as I could, then grabbed my cell from my pocket and dialed one of my contracted doctors on staff.

She answered immediately.

"Yeah, it's Matt," I sighed. "I'm going to need you to come in tomorrow morning, first thing. I need a full physical and drug test. Yeah, new client. I think she might be doping."

Chapter Ten

I woke up feeling like a million pounds of trash had been stuffed into a semi and frozen with water and then rolled over my body several times before pinning me down.

Maybe that was a little exaggerated, but I was sore everywhere. My mouth even hurt, though I think that had to do more with clenching my teeth than anything. I'd thought the run home would make the panic go away, and then I realized that I'd left everything in my bag, and I do mean everything. Even when I didn't take any of the pills, I kept them with me at all times, just in case.

I'd been trying to wean myself off them for the last two months, but the nightmares still came.

It was the only thing that kept the monsters away when it got real bad.

Thankfully, when I got back to my room my bag was sitting on my bed as if it had been there the whole time.

Everything locked up tight.

I'd breathed a sigh of relief and promptly taken a shower, ready to face the next day of training with all the enthusiasm of getting a root canal.

Don't get me wrong, I loved soccer.

But the training part? Where my muscles hurt so bad I was afraid I was going to have a problem sitting on the toilet? Not my favorite part.

I winced as I sat up in bed and then slowly pulled my feet over the side, trying not to inhale too deeply, since it hurt to breathe. I walked like a grandma to the shower and searched for some Tiger Balm to rub on my body. I barely got one cupboard open before I heard his voice.

"Looking for something?"

"Your whistle," I said with a hiss. "So I can flush it down the toilet."

"I sleep with it under my pillow, and I have a spare."

"Now that's a dream come true."

"What?" I could feel him behind me.

I turned. "Strangling you with the whistle cord while you sleep."

His lips twitched. "Doubt you're strong enough, but you're welcome to try."

"Don't tempt me." I tried not to slump, didn't want to show any weakness as his eyes raked over me. "Did you need something? Other than some morning banter to go with your coffee?"

"Sore?"

"You have no idea."

"I bet I do." He looked behind me like he was searching for something and then faced me again. "You've got your physical first thing this morning and then we train some more. Your tryout for the Reign is set for next weekend."

"Two weeks!" I yelled. "Actually we have less than two weeks!"

"I'll get you there," he said softly. "Just remember you have to do your part too."

"My spleen did its part yesterday," I grumbled. "Trust me."

"Can I?" He seemed surprised that he'd said it as he narrowed his eyebrows and brushed a hand through his thick beautiful hair. "Can I trust you?"

I gulped. "Can I trust you?"

"That doesn't work with me. You can't answer a question with a question. Can I trust you? Taking you on could ruin my reputation, you know."

"Or it could make you a genius for signing the highest-paid female soccer player in the world?" I offered lamely.

His eyes drilled holes into me. "Don't make an ass out of yourself, out of us, alright?"

Us? What was this *us* business? I was about to say something when a knock sounded at the door.

My tongue suddenly felt thick as I remembered my last physical . . . Focus. I could do this. I could do this.

"I hope you don't mind, but we'll be doing a drug test as well," Matt said flippantly as he left the bathroom.

Hands shaking, I felt tears well in my eyes.

The universe was against me.

Or maybe it was just powerful men with too much of everything going for them who were out to get me.

Or consume me.

Control me.

Own me.

I clenched my hands into fists and followed him out into the living room expecting the worst, when I saw a really pretty older lady with cheerful eyes and silver streaks through her black hair. "You must be Parker!" She walked up to me like she knew me, pulled me in for a hug, and then grabbed my hand and started walking me away from Matt.

Was this normal?

He was looking at his phone.

Hello, stranger danger!

I mean I could take her but . . .

"My name's April." She grinned. "This will be fast and easy. It always is. I've been working with Matt for the last few years, love his clients, and you look delightful." Was this the part where she pinched my cheek and offered me a Ricola?

Before I knew it, the elderly woman in the black pantsuit with the pretty gold earrings was shoving me into the bathroom with a little cup. "We do this for every client."

I bet they did.

It wasn't unusual.

It still made me sweat.

For reasons I couldn't talk about.

With shaking hands I took the cup, closed the door, and leaned against it as I let another tear fall before I walked over to the toilet and laughed at my predicament. That guy was a total ass, wasn't he? I could barely even hover over the bowl and now I had to try to pee in a cup without my legs giving out on me?

Hilarious.

It took me at least ten seconds to get into position, and when everything was over, my legs were burning so much it felt like someone had lit them on fire and then done it again just to be sure they had enough to roast a marshmallow.

I winced, screwed the top on the cup, and then left it on the counter and made my way back out to the living room, where Willow was eating breakfast and Matt seemed to be stewing on the phone again.

"Alright, dear." April walked past me and into the bathroom. I went in search of some orange juice. Within five minutes, April was escorting me back into the bathroom and doing her physical, checking each part of me and then pulling out a tourniquet. "I need to take some blood and then we're all through!"

"I hate needles," I confessed.

"Don't we all?" She just laughed. "You sit on the stool right there, and I'll tell you a Matt story about when he was little and refused to get a shot for pneumonia."

I sat immediately. "You knew him when he was little?"

She scrunched up her nose. "Of course, he's my grandson."

"Wait, what?" I almost shot out of my chair except I was so sore I couldn't move. "His grandmother, but you work for him?"

"Private contractor. I retired from the hospital several years ago and make house calls in my free time. I like to travel, so it works for me." She pulled out a needle and a few vials.

I gulped.

"He was ornery when he was young. He's just angry now." Her laugh was infectious and light as she put on gloves then grabbed a cotton ball and rubbed a spot on my inner elbow. "Once, when he was fifteen, he got sicker than a dog. I told him he needed a shot in his bum and he said he'd rather die, so I told him I would give him two Snickers if he got on his hands and knees and let me stick him."

I burst out laughing, despite the fear trickling down my spine. "You asked to stick him?" I could only imagine what Matt thought of that, and visions of a handsome teen too cocky for his own good entered my mind. I tried to focus on that, focus on that image of innocence. I would have had the same reaction as a teen. I didn't have time to be sick because there was soccer and friends and all the things an angsty teen focuses on instead of the real world. Spring days filled with training and laughter, the smell of fresh-cut grass, and people cheering. And then, all of those things started to get mixed in with right and wrong, and crossing boundaries, lines. They were mixed in with tears and sweat and anger and shame.

I swallowed the soccer ball of shame lodged in my throat, and tried to keep my expression happy and my mouth wide instead of lips tightly pressed together, ready to lash out at anything and anyone who looked at me wrong. It was so much easier being angry than being afraid, wasn't it?

"He was mortified." April giggled. I hoped I didn't look like I felt: faint and probably pale. "Mainly because I did it in front of his two friends." She shrugged. "I figured I'd get him in the exam room one of two ways: embarrassment over his crazy grandma, or chocolate."

"Smart," I managed to choke out.

"He took the shot, and I gave him a sticker with a naked chicken on it that said *I've been shot*. I think he's kept it to this day." She grinned wide and then patted my leg. "Alright, now I'm going to stick you." She followed that statement with a wink. "But I'm very gentle. Tell me about yourself."

"I love soccer." I started with the truth so she wouldn't see past the forced smile on my lips or the way I shook whenever I thought about all the memories linked to soccer, the ones that made me afraid. I hated fear more than I hated the shame that was chained to it like a heavy pile of bricks with all of my insecurities scribbled across them in angry black letters.

"Obviously you love soccer." The first prick of the needle had my body feeling ill as I squeezed my eyes shut.

"He put me through a lot of training yesterday."

"Who? Your new coach?" How much blood did the woman need?

"What? No." I licked my dry lips. "I meant Matt."

Ten vials? Was she taking ten vials?

I swayed a bit.

"Oh," was her answer. "I mean, that's interesting. In all my years, I've never seen Matt coach one of his clients. He typically pays a trainer . . . something about not getting involved in the specifics."

My eyes shot open. "Really?" Why did that make my stomach drop? What was it about me? Or was he just that concerned I wasn't going to make the cut?

"Maybe he just has a vested interest in the pretty ones." I knew she meant it as a compliment, but the compliment went right past my ears, stabbed me in the heart, and whispered one thing and one thing only.

"That's all you'll ever be good for . . ."

The cruel smile.

The smell of peppermint and antiseptic.

"All done!" she announced, placing a blue bandage on my arm. "You can go now, careful as you get up, and for your trouble . . ." She produced a red lollipop that made me nostalgic all over again.

It was a disorienting feeling. Wishing for the past, hating my present, terrified of the future, holding a lollipop between my fingers like it was the only thing I could trust to be real.

I tugged the wrapper off and stuck it in my mouth before I burst into tears, and she squeezed my hand and said, "It's going to be okay."

I almost confessed it all.

Almost.

Nobody had gotten in.

And yet a friendly doctor almost did it with a short talk and a sucker.

Or maybe I was the sucker in this scenario.

I made my way back into the living room and found Matt freshly showered and on his phone again. Surprise, surprise.

"No! I said no! No parties and I don't care whose birthday—" He growled. "Why do you do these things to me? Fine, fine, just nothing late, I know your schedule this week. At least now I can babysit you morons." He hung up.

Willow was stretched across the couch with a blanket over her legs, flipping through the channels on TV, and I was suddenly frozen as a shiver wracked my body.

Matt narrowed his eyes on me, and the beauty of them terrified me. Was he friend or foe? Enemy or worse? "You look rough."

"Nice." I snorted. "At least I got a sucker for good behavior. That's much better than a lame sticker, hmm?"

He glared. "Using my childhood against me gets you nowhere."

"Fine," I bit out. "I think I'm just going to go lie down."

"Good idea." His gaze didn't waver. "I'm going to ask you again, Parker, is there anything I should know? As your agent? As the guy saving your ass this season? Anything at all that you haven't told me?"

My throat all but closed up as I shook my head slowly and whispered, "Nothing you need to know."

"That's not the same thing."

"It's all you're going to get." I turned on my heel and walked off, then shut the door quietly behind me, lay against it, and slid to the floor as tears dripped from my face.

Chapter Eleven

MATT

Lately I'd been on edge without anything to alleviate the anxiety rippling through me.

For starters my sister was currently flirting with Jagger over a bottle of Heineken, stars in her eyes, and wearing a short dress that I'm 99 percent sure was supposed to be a tank top—for a preteen.

Problem number two was Jagger's bad-boy reputation paired with his grandmother, who still managed to be headline news even after charges weren't pressed against her.

And then there was Parker.

She hadn't come out of her room since April's visit.

And normally I wouldn't have minded, but it was loud, very loud in the house. Music pumped out of every Bose speaker I owned, drinks were flowing. All in all, it was a controlled party but a party nonetheless.

I burned a hole through the wall several times with my stare just willing her to get up and make an appearance so I knew she was okay.

Which also pissed me off because she wasn't mine to check up on.

And I was surrounded by pretty women on a daily basis.

But none of them played soccer the way she did.

With pure joy.

With die-hard focus.

One thing was for certain: after today, I at least knew she had extraordinary talent, so why the hell throw it away over a bad attitude? Over an asshole coach?

I took another draw of beer just as Slade Rodriguez walked up. "Heard you just moved into coaching?"

Great, another client feeling the need to chime in with an interest in my job. I rolled my eyes. "Short notice, we have less than two weeks to get her into shape so I took on the job."

He saw right through my bullshit. His creepy golden-brown eyes narrowed in on me just as his wife flashed a wave our way. "Why don't I believe you? I mean, under fourteen days? You're Matt Kingston, couldn't you just pick up the phone permanently attached to your hand and make a call?"

I gulped. "Maybe."

"Beep. Wrong answer. The answer is 'Well, of course, Slade, but I like watching her run in—'"

"Client," I choked out, taking another swig of beer. "Also my sister's age, so . . . off-limits."

"Why's that?" He crossed his arms.

"Look, you met her, she needed my help, and if it wasn't for your *wife* . . ." I smiled and waved at her. I loved her, but she had thrown me under the bus when she asked me to take on Parker as a client. "I wouldn't be in this position."

My attention was suddenly stolen by a girl with auburn, honeyed locks wearing short white shorts, a black tank, and gray Converse making her way out of her bedroom and into the party, smiling.

"Yeah, just keep telling yourself that, bro." Slade patted me on the back. "And I'll be here when you cry into your bottle of wine."

"I'm not as lame as you." I laughed and then gulped back two more swigs. "Plus, she's not my type."

He followed my gaze, seeing the same perfect tits, long muscular legs, and gorgeous hair with a makeup-free face and easy white smile as I did. "Riiight."

I rolled my eyes and went in search of another beer. In the kitchen I watched Jagger with murder in my eyes as he wrapped an arm around Willow and whispered something in her ear.

"I think they're hooking up," came Parker's amused voice.

I turned slowly and pried the beer from her hands. "No drinking during training."

"Hey!" She put her hands on her hips while I took a long, searing sip and stupidly wondered if she'd already pressed her lips against the bottle. And as luck would have it, Slade chose that moment to wink at me from across the room.

Was everyone against me?

Parker scowled. "I can have one beer."

"Not with my training, Cheetah Girl. I bet you hurt everywhere . . ." I actually enjoyed the look of fury on her face as she tucked her hair behind her ears and stared me down.

"Not that it's any of your business, but my muscles have muscles that are sore. You're evil, and why are you even training me? April said you don't train your clients."

Caught.

I looked down and shrugged like it didn't matter, like I couldn't smell her perfume, like I wasn't aching to feel her tan legs wrapped around me. God, I really was an asshole, wasn't I?

"I didn't have time to get anyone else." I forced a smile. "Besides, my usual trainer made the last guy cry and he was over three hundred pounds. I thought I'd give you a break."

"Bet you could make anyone cry," she fired back.

"Is that what you want?" I asked curiously. "For such crippling pain and soreness that you cry yourself to sleep?"

She hissed out a breath. "I could take it."

"Bet you could," I said, seriously watching her swollen mouth suck in a few shallow breaths as I cornered her against the pantry door. "But unless you do something to really piss me off, you won't ever have to suffer like that."

"I piss you off by existing."

"Because you're immature and spoiled," I answered honestly. "Because you took an opportunity people would kill for and let your anger rule you."

"Wow." She smiled brightly. It was insincere, and I hated it. "Must be nice to have all the answers, know everything. How's that working out for you?"

I spread my arms wide. "That's pretty obvious, isn't it?"

She bit down on her bottom lip, all traces of her smile gone. "Yeah. Totally obvious."

She reached past me for a bottle of water just as Willow approached. "You're up!"

"Yay." Parker made a motion with her hands and popped open the water, droplets slid down her neck as she took a huge gulp. Two Sounders players behind her gawked like horny college students. I quelled them with a fierce glare. They held up their hands and looked away but not before glancing back one last time.

Idiots.

My phone buzzed in my pocket.

Finally.

I moved to the corner of the kitchen and answered. "April, what's the verdict?"

"Well, she's healthy as a horse, that's for sure." I gripped the phone tighter.

"Yeah, I figured that, what about everything else?"

"Blood test checked out. She did have some higher levels of benzodiazepine in her urine."

Disappointment hit me in the chest, disappointment and anger. "You're sure?"

"I'm positive, but Matt, that doesn't mean—"

"Thanks, April."

I hung up the phone as red filled my line of vision.

Did she think she could take advantage of me?

My hospitality?

My family?

My time?

My training?

I stomped over to her. "We need to talk."

Parker gave me a funny look then smiled. "Okay, then talk."

"Not here."

"Matt—"

I grabbed her by the wrist, causing her to spill water all over the kitchen floor. She stumbled behind me. "Let me go!"

"Stop being so unreasonable!" I snapped.

"Please, I can't, please, just please . . ." The only thing that made me let her go was the fact that she sounded afraid, not angry or unreasonable, but afraid. I released her, chest heaving as I pressed her body against the wall.

She squeezed her eyes shut like I was going to hit her.

What the hell was going on?

I backed up, tried to cool myself down, and then said through clenched teeth, "You lied to me."

Her eyes flashed open. "Excuse me?"

"You. Lied."

"About what?" By the pale look on her face, I knew I was right. I knew she'd been hiding shit, but drugs? Really?

"You. Tell. Me." People were starting to stare. I could feel their eyes on my back as I held her in the corner, judging her, needing her to tell me it was a false positive, needing her to tell me she wasn't just going to throw away her entire career for quick, happy, feel-good moments.

She gulped. "I really don't know."

"Stop fucking lying to me! If you can't trust me, I can't help you! Your drug test popped positive!"

I didn't mean to raise my voice. I'd like to think it was disappointment raging, but it was more than that, it was being let down by someone I wanted to succeed, someone who gave me a reason to believe that everyone else was wrong and she was right. And I hated that I trusted and was wrong. I hated fucking being wrong.

Her eyes widened. "That's it?"

"What the hell do you mean *that's it?*" I threw my hands in the air. "You can't just pop positive on a drug test and play professional ball!"

"I'm on antianxiety meds, you jackass!" she snarled. "I've never popped positive on a drug test because I haven't needed them until this last year! I didn't even think about it, okay?"

"What?" I backed up.

Tears filled her eyes as the party fell tense and quiet.

"I have anxiety." A tear spilled over her cheek. "I take Xanax when the panic attacks get really bad, but as long as I train really hard I'm usually okay. Except lately . . ."

"Lately I've been pushing you too hard?" I wondered out loud. "Lately . . . what? You have to communicate with me!"

She started to walk away.

Seriously? Who parented this woman!

I followed her all the way into her bedroom, not caring who saw. It didn't matter. She was a client, and I'd done worse with other clients. Hell, I used to follow Slade into the bathroom.

"You can't just walk away from me the way you do your problems!" I yelled, slamming the door behind us. "I'm the only person on your side right now. If you need pills, tell me why. If you need help, tell me you need it. If you need ice, you yell at me to get you fucking ice. You can't just run, Parker. Not here. Not now."

She sat down on the bed, bowing her head, defeated. "Running's the only way to escape . . . did you know that?"

"Why the hell would you want to escape all of this?"

"How old are you?"

"What the—"

"Just answer the question. I know it's stupid, just answer."

"Thirty," I breathed out and knelt in front of her. "What's this all about? I know I'm tough on you, but if you think shit is hard now, try when you have a million cameras in your face, when you're on a Wheaties box with an Olympic gold medal and you have little girls looking up to you wanting your autograph, when you have people saying they want to grow up and be just like you, that's when shit gets hard. This, this is easy."

She was quiet, and then, "I'm afraid."

"It's okay to be afraid."

"Not of fame." She finally met my gaze. Her pretty brown eyes were filled with tears threatening to spill over, her hands were clutched together in her lap, and her jaw was clenched. "I don't like dark rooms. They set me off. So does the smell of peppermint. And older guys looking at me like they want me to take my shirt off. Actually, these days any guy looking at me makes me panic. I just . . . I'm okay with the soccer stuff. But being touched, being stared at, cornered, anything that makes me feel unsafe . . . So yes I've been taking a lot of Xanax lately, to sleep. To keep me from dark places with hollow laughter, rough hands, and the smell of gum."

I ran my hands through my hair and then placed my hands on hers. "There's more to this than I know?"

She nodded.

"Does Willow know?"

She shook her head.

"Does anyone know?"

She just shrugged.

"Okay, so apparently we aren't talking about dark corners and peppermint gum, not today. But one day, you're going to need to trust someone enough to tell them so that the nightmares stop, so that the lashing out stops, so that you take control of your life again."

"Control." She laughed like it was funny. "It's not real, is it?"

"You decide that," I said softly. "And make me one promise."

Our eyes locked.

Off-limits. She's off-limits.

I just never realized how much.

"Don't yell at me. Talk to me, like your agent, like your coach, like your friend."

She smiled at that.

"Use your words nicely, so I know how to make sure you succeed, alright?"

"I thought you weren't my friend."

Silence settled between us as I thought about the times she'd lashed out. It wasn't anger talking—it was fear. Protectiveness crashed over me hard and fast.

"Things change," I said as I stood, wanting to do nothing more than wrap my arms around her and ask who hurt her so I could hurt them. "I think you need a friend who isn't Willow."

Her laugh made me smile. "She's a good friend."

"She's manipulative."

"In the best of ways." Parker beamed up at me. "Otherwise, I wouldn't have met you."

"You can't say things like that to me. I don't know what to do when you're being nice."

"Likewise."

We stared for a few more minutes, me trying to figure her out, and her probably trying to decide if she really could trust me.

A knock sounded at the door, and Willow poked her head in. "Everything okay after that yelling match?"

"Yeah." I nodded.

"Yup," Parker agreed. "I'm just going to go to bed."

"Okay." Willow sent me a seething glare as I followed her out, and just as I was about to turn off the light, I reached for the lamp, turned it on, then turned off the master light.

From her expression, you'd think I'd just given her gold.

Parker mouthed *"Thank you."*

I shut the door behind me and suddenly felt older than my thirty years.

On one hand she was this courageous, talented woman; on the other hand, she seemed like she'd jump if she saw her own shadow.

I felt her relax when we talked.

Saw it on her face.

I wanted her to see herself the way the world would see her: talented, beautiful.

With a sigh I ran my hands through my hair again and wondered how I could save her when she refused to be the girl who needed saving.

She had lifeboats surrounding her and yet she was still drowning. I could try to be one of those lifeboats . . . or I could end up sinking right along with her.

Chapter Twelve

PARKER

I woke up and got dressed in my workout gear then nearly tripped over something left in front of my door.

It was a stuffed dinosaur.

The note pinned to it said *To chase the darkness away.* —*Matt*

I smiled so big you'd think someone had just given me a million dollars. I couldn't remember the last time I'd slept with a stuffed animal. My throat closed up as I set it on top of my made bed with a smile, ready to take a picture and send it to Willow to brag that someone had given me something so wonderful.

Except what would I say?

Your brother got me a dinosaur because I opened up to him about some fears, no big deal?

She'd pry.

And she already knew that I refused to speak about that day. Would she be hurt to know that I opened up even just a little to Matt?

If you had told me a week ago I would talk to him about anything, I would have laughed my ass off.

Now I felt . . . freer, like saying the words didn't damn me as much as I thought they would. Instead, we'd shared a smile, and I'd stupidly thought about his smile all night, and the way he touched my leg, not like he was ready to pounce but like he genuinely wanted to make sure that I was okay.

It had been a long time since I'd been touched out of care.

And I liked it a lot.

Amazing what human kindness does to someone with so many scars.

I shut my door quietly and made my way into the bathroom. The light was on, the door open.

And as luck would have it, Matt was shirtless, brushing his teeth like it was normal for me to walk in on him without him yelling profanities or using all the hot water.

I stopped in the doorway.

He narrowed his eyes.

I narrowed mine and crossed my arms.

And then he spit into the sink and rinsed it down, wiped his mouth with the towel, and turned toward me. I saw nothing but muscled abs and a tan that looked way too real to be anything but.

With a twitch of his lips, he grabbed my toothbrush, sauntered toward me, then stopped. My breath stalled in my lungs as he held it out to me.

"Be ready in five."

I nodded dumbly as I took it from his hands then stupidly called after his retreating back, "Thanks for the dinosaur!"

He stopped walking, shook his head, and then kept going.

When I turned to look in the mirror, my face was flushed like I'd just run drills for five hours, and my hand shook as I tried to put toothpaste on the bristles.

And when I looked back in the mirror.

I smiled.

Thanks for the dinosaur?

Good one, Parker. Good one.

◆　◆　◆

"Why are you smiling at me like that?" Matt yelled as I ran another lap then hit the cones, dribbling between them before hitting the ball in his direction in order to score.

"Just." I sucked in a breath. "Imagining." Make it through the cones, and last one, break out. "Strangling you." Aim. Kick. Goal! "In your sleep!"

"Again." He grinned, tossing me the ball.

"See?" I went through that same drill another ten times, until he had every move in my arsenal memorized, meaning basically no more goals on my end and more running instead.

He blew his whistle.

"Oh, thank God." I bent over and tried to suck in air while I watched his cleats walk past me as he grabbed a few more balls. "Wait, what are you doing? We've been at this for three hours."

"One-on-one," he answered.

I held in my groan and made my way over to him, my legs wobbly and tired, so sore and heavy I wanted to take a long nap on the cool green turf. Instead, I had five balls in front of me and an evil coach with a red whistle that I was going to flush down the toilet later.

Sweat dripped down my face, and I wiped my eyes with my sleeves.

"Got a little something right here." He pointed at the sweat on my chin.

I gave him a middle finger.

"Ah, that's the spirit," he chuckled. "Alright, beat me and you can go home."

"Wait, that's it? I just have to beat you?"

"You're warm, I'm not."

"You played pro. I'm trying to get in." I bent over and examined the goal, his posture, the way he looked at me, and down at the balls. "You're calculating."

"You're studying me." He grinned. "Won't make it easier."

"Injury," I said, snapping my fingers. "Which knee was it?"

"Not telling." He kicked the ball to me, and I stopped it with my foot. "Besides, I knew I couldn't cut it, not like the other guys. Some of us have it, others are better on the sidelines."

"I've got it," I said confidently.

"Then show me." His gaze was unwavering. I'd never actually had a coach challenge me. I was their star player, and they just wanted points up on the board. They wanted to fill the stadium's seats.

And I did that, did it and more.

And all it got me was panic attacks, bad memories, and kicked out of my favorite sport.

"Hey." Matt clapped his hands twice. "Focus or I'm pulling out the whistle again."

I growled, which only made him laugh.

I dribbled left, right, through his feet, and thought I was home free until he kicked the ball from behind me, tangling me up in his legs and sending me slamming down to the ground. He stuck out a hand to help me up. "Four more left."

"What happens after four?"

He smirked. "You don't want to know."

Shit!

I dribbled toward him this time, aggressively going to the left before I faked right and kicked. I missed the goal, but at least he didn't steal the ball from me this time.

"Three," he said like I couldn't count.

I hesitated and watched his face as I started the third run toward him, and when I faked, I went back to the same side. This time he caught me, and I slammed into his chest, taking us both to the ground.

Sweat dripped from my chin onto his. I grinned and touched the place it splashed. "Got a little something right here."

"Smart-ass." He didn't move. "Two balls left."

"You'll let me know the feeling of only having one, right?" I looked down just as he shoved me off him then stood and begrudgingly helped me to my feet.

"I could do a hell of a lot with one, trust me."

I gasped.

"One soccer ball," he clarified, hitting me with his shoulder as he walked past and took his stance.

I rolled my eyes and chased after him, then stared at the ball, then at him again. He was expecting me to dribble toward him.

Not to just kick the ball.

He was standing a few feet away.

I frowned.

He grinned like he knew where my head was at.

So I took a few steps, faked a kick, dribbled to the right, and kicked a perfect goal that went sailing into the net.

His applause mixed with my joy that I did it with one ball left. Without thinking, I ran full speed at him and jumped into his arms.

He swung me around like he expected it.

Then, as if he realized he was holding me, he quickly dropped me to my feet and held up his hand for a high five. "Good read, Parker. You finally saw the play. You don't have to dribble every time. Sometimes it's just as easy as kicking the ball."

I put my hands on my hips as I contemplated what he said. "You were far enough away, I was just making it harder on myself."

"You were thinking here." He tapped my temple. "Instead of here." He tapped my chest. It was just one finger, but I felt it. Man, did I feel it all the way down to my toes.

Every coach I'd had . . . had babied me.

He made me want to find a sharp object and aim for his man parts.

There was something to be said about a coach earning your respect, and he'd just earned mine. Big time.

"Thanks." I looked down.

"Let's go get you cleaned up. No way am I letting you in that SUV all sweaty."

"Hey!"

"Hey nothing, you're hitting the showers and then maybe I'll feed you."

"Best coach ever," I grumbled. "And agent."

"I kind of like being both."

"Because you like torturing people?" I joked as we grabbed the extra bag of balls and walked toward the locker rooms.

He grinned over at me. "Only you, it seems."

I handed him the balls. "Obviously." I pushed the metal door open. "Give me ten minutes?"

"Sure." He didn't look back. I just shrugged and went into the women's lockers, imagining the day I could put my gear in the shiny wood cupboards and sit in those cushy seats. When I'd see my name above one of the lockers.

It finally felt like it could happen.

That maybe I could escape my past.

I dropped my gear onto the ground and turned on one of the showers, kicked off my cleats, pulled off my shin guards and socks, then stripped, all before diving under the hot water.

It felt amazing.

I rubbed the water down my body, then quickly went over to my bag to grab one of my spare towels and soap. I always kept shower stuff in my duffel just in case. I didn't have nice shampoo, mostly travel gear, but it was enough to get the smell of sweat out of my skull and off my body.

I wanted to stay there forever.

Probably would have been tempted.

But the lights flickered.

And then turned completely off.

Panic hit me so hard I tripped over my own feet and landed on my ass in an effort to hurl myself into the corner.

"Matt!" I yelled, my voice weak and fearful like I was too afraid to even scream. "Matt!"

Frantic, I tried standing, but my sore legs gave out on me as I wrapped my arms around them and rested my trembling chin on my knees.

"Parker?" Matt's voice sounded worried. "Are you okay? Parker?"

"Here," I whispered and then louder: "Here."

The shower was still on. I was afraid to turn it off, afraid to move. It was dark, so dark.

I rocked back and forth, teeth chattering, and not just because of the cold water.

"Parker?" His voice was closer as a body rounded the corner, cell phone high in the air. Why hadn't I thought of that?

"Yeah."

"The power's out because of the rain. Are you done showering?"

"Yes." Teeth chattering, I tried to stand on unsteady legs and fell down. "Ouch!"

"Are you hurt?" His voice was more frantic this time.

"Only my ass. My pride. And my body from my masochistic coach," I mumbled under my breath as I heard the water cut off and then saw sandals and jogger pants appear in front of me. It was too dark to see anything else, and I was afraid to look up.

Without warning, I was being helped to my feet and wrapped in the towel I had set down on the bench. "You're okay."

How had he known I wasn't?

I clung to him, wet from the shower, towel barely covering my body, my mind at war with itself. Why did I trust him? I shouldn't. He was dangerous. But he showed me that he cared. And I respected him.

Another chill wracked my body. He wrung out my wet hair and then pried my hands from him and wrapped the towel tightly around my body. "I'll turn around while you get dressed, okay? Just tell me if you need more light." He handed me his cell.

He didn't even look at me.

Not like last time.

Last time he'd looked at me like he wanted to punish me.

This time, his voice was raspy.

With a bit of concern.

And something else that I wasn't sure I could identify.

Which in turn made me shake as I dressed quickly and then handed his cell phone back. "Ready."

"Good." He wrapped an arm around me and guided me out of the still-dark building. Rain pounded over both of us as we ran to his SUV.

"Guess I didn't need that shower," I joked once we were inside with the smell of expensive leather filling the air.

He stared at me as he pressed the ignition. His gaze raked over me slowly, warming me from the inside out. "Guess not."

And that was it. We drove home in silence.

And when we walked into the house, I didn't miss the fact that he had his hand on my lower back the entire way.

And I'd bet money he didn't even realize he'd been doing it.

Chapter Thirteen

MATT

I had a shit day ahead of me, ending with more practice that evening with Parker. I hated to admit it, but I looked forward to our time together, and the worst part was she wasn't just off-limits because of who I was, she was off-limits because of something that had happened to her, something bad.

I replayed images of the terror on her face in the locker room and felt even more like a jackass that I'd treated her so horribly.

Irony reared its ugly head. How many times had I told Slade not to be a jackass when Mack worked for him? How many times did I send flowers on his behalf? And this was what I learned? To go the jackass route like he had? To forget that I was dealing with another human being with their own thoughts and feelings?

Great.

I glanced around my office. Light flooded in through the sliding glass door, spotlighting my bookcase, pictures of me at the ESPYs with Slade and Jagger on the top shelf, and awards right below it. So many awards, medals, things, and yet there I sat, soccer ball in hand, wondering what the hell I was going to do about Parker. About the fear. I wanted to help, to shove it away, to pull her into my arms, and there it was again.

I wanted to touch her.

But touching her was off-limits. The woman was petrified of the dark, would she have the same reaction to me?

I tossed the soccer ball in the air again just as the door to my office flew open. "Guess what!" Willow clapped her hands and then dragged Parker in behind her. Parker had a can of potato chips open and was currently licking her fingers. Disgusting. Alluring. Sexy as hell. Damn it!

I nodded to the chips and then reached into my desk and tossed her a packet of whey protein.

She handed me the chips with a pissed-off look and scrunched up her nose at the protein pack. *Peanut butter. Yum.* I knew firsthand it was the worst flavor, and apparently she did too.

"What?" I finally said, acknowledging my sister, who was still able to bounce from stiletto to stiletto without spraining an ankle. She was wearing black leggings and a tank, making workout leisure look a hell of a lot more leisure. I'd be shocked if she could dribble a ball.

"So the LA team, whatever their name is, tried to reach you." I sighed in annoyance. "Whatever, I'll learn the names of all the teams, and balls, and yay, sports! Anyways, I was just too excited. Apparently they caught wind of Parker's tryout for the Seattle Reign and said they'd be interested in a meeting. They heard something about an attitude transformation and wanted to see if it was true."

"Attitude transformation?" Parker huffed. "I have a great personality."

"When you're not sticking your foot up people's asses, some might say *shining*." I winked.

She stuck out her tongue.

We smiled at each other a minute before my sister waved her hand in front of my face. "Matt? Hello? They want you both to fly out tomorrow!"

"Tomorrow!" Parker screeched.

"Tomorrow." Willow did a little wiggle with her hips. "It's perfect. I can hold down the fort here, you guys take the first flight out after practice. It's a short flight anyway, stay the night and—"

"She's not ready," I interrupted.

"What?" both girls yelled in unison. I had half a mind to grab the ibuprofen from my right drawer and chew it dry. The voices, so loud, always so damn loud.

"She's doing great!" Willow insisted.

"I'm working my ass off!" said Parker, glaring at me.

"See?" Willow pointed at her. "She's ready!" She slapped Parker's ass. Parker winced. "Ouch."

"Sorry." Willow rubbed it, right in front of me, sparking some weird sinful envy inside as I shook my head at both girls.

Parker had excitement in her eyes, and Willow went back to hopping on both feet.

If she clapped, I was going for the ibuprofen.

Hell, if she screamed or said *yay* in that high-pitched voice I was going for something stronger, like whiskey.

"Fine," I grumbled. "Willow, make yourself useful and get the flight and hotel booked. Double-check with the LA team, also known as the Fliers." I said it slowly, hoping it would stick, but hell, who was I kidding? My sister only listened when she wanted to. "Find out their schedule, and get us a dinner booked, no tryouts. We're just there to talk stats."

"Yes!" she squealed. Wasn't as bad as a *yay*, but I still winced as she ran out the door, leaving me and Parker alone.

"You really think I'm ready?" She plopped down into a seat and put her feet up on my desk. Her brown hair was down again, kissing her bare shoulders and making her look more approachable than normal. The familiarity was going to kill me—it already *was*.

I flicked her Converse with my pen and shook my head. "As long as you keep your feet off the table, dress your age, and try not to burp during dinner I think we'll be okay."

She made a face. "I know how to be a lady."

"You have a chip." I nodded toward her chest. "On your shirt right there."

She pulled her feet from my desk and pointed her finger at me. "I'm going to impress the hell out of them. You won't even recognize me."

And for some reason, that made me sad. "Parker," I called as she started stomping out of my office. "Don't change who you are . . ." I cleared my throat as her face softened. "Maybe just . . . polish up a bit . . ."

She was almost out of my office when I laughed to myself.

"What?" She poked her head back in.

"You have Pringles in your hair."

"Son of a bitch!" She marched off yelling.

And I held back my tongue. What I was going to say? My confession? You're more beautiful with a Pringle in your hair than you are with a fancy blowout?

I liked messy Parker.

Messy Parker was real.

I wasn't sure I would survive any other type, because she had me hungry for more. Hell, I was already fantasizing, already wanting what I knew I had to keep at arm's length.

Parker acting like a foul-mouthed lady might just set me off.

I reached for the ibuprofen.

And quickly bypassed it for the whiskey.

Chapter Fourteen

I wasn't the type to take selfies.

But I had a pod.

In first class.

So I took ten.

Much to Matt's dismay, I kept snapping photos of everything from the plug-ins to the special eye mask they gave me along with a wine list and appetizer list.

"You travel like this all the time?" I put my feet up on the little stool that only first-class people had and waited.

Matt set his phone down next to me and motioned for the flight attendant. "Whiskey neat."

"And what will you have, miss?" The flight attendants on Delta were all dressed in pretty purple dresses that almost looked out of place.

"Water," Matt answered for me.

I gave him a pleading look.

"And a light beer," he added, "with lime."

"Beer?" I hissed under my breath when she left.

"Beer helps your muscles, liquor just makes you dehydrated. Not that beer doesn't, but it does help recovery, and you limped like Quasimodo all the way through security."

"Glad you noticed. Not enough ibuprofen in the world when it comes to you, Matt Kingston."

"And not enough whiskey in the world when living with you," he said sarcastically. "Put your phone down. People are staring, and usually I fly private."

I almost dropped my phone. "Private, as in, just you?"

"Yes." He thanked the flight attendant as she handed us our drinks.

"Wait, like just you, the pilots, and—"

"A flight crew, that's it."

"How much does that cost?"

"More than your college degree, why?" He grinned. "It's part of the lifestyle."

"Oh." Suddenly insecure, I put my phone down and looked around, wondering what everyone's jobs were, if I was even capable of living the sort of lifestyle where people recognized me.

And then there was Matt.

I knew he was loaded.

But reading about it and experiencing it were two very different things, weren't they? Because when you read about it, your imagination is never as good as the reality, is it?

Like I thought first class just included free drinks and bigger seats.

I was wrong.

And as I watched more and more people laugh over champagne, talk on their cell phones, open up their fancy computers, and ask the flight attendant to put away their nice jackets—I knew I was in over my head.

What was I thinking?

I was an athlete.

I didn't do polish.

I did nice, tight college-girl dresses and sneakers.

Panic overwhelmed me as I gripped the armrests.

"Parker?" Matt's low voice was soothing as I felt his touch on the back of my hand. It was warm, strong. Without thinking, I flipped my hand over and interlocked our fingers.

He squeezed tightly as I exhaled.

"What's going on in that head of yours?" he whispered as my heart thumped against my chest loud enough for everyone in the cabin to hear. I just wasn't sure if it was the fact that I could hold his hand and not have a panic attack, feel his warmth and like it (love it?), or that I'd suddenly come to the conclusion that I didn't just need his help getting the attention of a team, I needed his help getting and keeping the team. Period.

I swallowed the dryness in my throat.

My pride.

And slowly turned my head to the right. His eyes were always so blue, so stark against his light hair and easy all-American smile. But he wasn't smiling now—no, he looked concerned, the man wasn't even blinking.

I opened my mouth. "I think I need more polish."

The corners of his mouth lifted up at the sides, giving him a boyish look. "Like nail polish or *polish* polish?"

"Oh no! I didn't even paint my nails! Do I need to paint my nails? Are they going to notice that I'm not—"

Matt's free hand covered my mouth in a manner that would have normally set me off, but the way his eyes drilled into me, the warmth from his body, even the way he smelled, like something rich and elegant, and all I kept thinking about was the cologne guys wore in high school that made you sniff just a little bit harder, it was that but refined, not overwhelming. And I didn't feel manhandled by him, more like he was trying to calm me down the only way he knew how.

"I don't like polish," he whispered. "Fingernail polish, that is. Never have." His smirk grew into something more tantalizing, beautiful, his shining white teeth adding to the devastating effect that was Matt Kingston's face. I tried not to sigh.

I failed.

"Furthermore . . ." He pulled his hand away and gripped my chin between his thumb and forefinger. "You're an athlete. All the team cares about is your stats and that you're not a media risk and you're a hard worker. Just be you, Parker."

"A week ago, you would have said to be anyone but myself," I countered in a whisper.

His eyes lowered to my mouth then back up to my eyes. "A week ago, I judged you like everyone else."

"That's the problem." I felt my lower lip quiver. "All they know is what they've read, they don't know the truth, *you* don't know the truth."

"I know you work hard," he said quickly. "I know you let me drill you until you're exhausted and ready to burst into tears." He bit down on his bottom lip and looked away like he'd said something wrong. "I know I respect you as an athlete. And I know you want this more than anything."

Not more than anything.

I almost gasped.

Did I just think that?

It had been forever since I'd felt . . . since my heart had jolted like someone just brought me back to life.

I exhaled slowly. "Okay, so what do I do?"

His smile was bright. "Drink your beer."

"That's it?"

"Yeah, they're going to take it away before takeoff."

"Monsters," I grumbled to his laughter while I chugged the rest of the beer just in time for the flight attendant to stop by. I handed her the plastic cup as Matt's fingers grazed my right cheek.

I grabbed his hand at the same time, ready to swipe at the drop that had escaped my mouth.

And there we were. His hand pressed against my cheek. My hand covering his—again.

And me wanting nothing more than for the warmth to stay.

"You two," the flight attendant said as she collected Matt's plastic cup. "So adorable. How long have you been a couple?"

"Uhhhhhhh." I shook my head. "No, no, it's not, no, really, we're . . ."

"Friends." Matt finished with a shrug, pulling his hand away. "Best friends ever since I gave her that stuffed dinosaur."

I rolled my eyes while the flight attendant laughed and then winked at him. "I like stuffed animals."

Matt gripped my right arm, pinning me to my spot as he chuckled and said, "Duly noted."

She walked off.

I mentally wished a hundred curses on her and every stuffed animal in her life and then continued glaring until Matt cleared his throat.

"What?" I pulled away. "She was hitting on you in front of your . . . friend." I gulped. Saying it out loud, right, I was an idiot.

"She's clearly a monster who deserves to break out in hives." Matt nodded solemnly. "Relax, watch a movie, I'll catch up on work and make sure Willow hasn't bankrupted me."

"So many shoes, so little time." I laughed.

He stared at me, like really stared, like he was trying to see if I was being serious, and then he leaned in. "Do you like shoes?"

"Converse." I shrugged and grabbed my headphones. "I love Converse and Nikes. Heels are fine, but you can't run in heels. I mean I could if a bear was chasing me or if I was chasing a taco, but I'd prefer Converse."

"I mean heels can be useful. What if you were starving?" Matt joked. "You'd have to use your stilettos to kill your own food in the wild, versus wearing Converse and catching it."

"Exactly!" I threw my arms wide. "Why does nobody understand this?"

He held out his fist, I bumped it. "I get you."

"Yeah." The pitter-patter of my heart was back. "You do . . . when you're not yelling."

He opened up his computer.

"Or using your damn whistle," I muttered under my breath.

He leaned in, his lips caressing my ear, I think by accident. I think? "Don't make me pull it out."

I let out a weary sigh. What was happening to me? I couldn't calm the erratic beat of my heart any more than I could get a good deep breath in. "Bet you say that to all the girls."

Did I just say that out loud?

To my coach?

Friend?

Agent?

Well, good-bye, LA and Seattle. I was going to hell and getting dropped!

Matt burst out laughing, earning the attention of several people sitting in our area as the plane taxied the runway. "Yeah, I deserved that one."

"Totally." I exhaled in relief and stared wide-eyed down at my phone as I tried to find a song, any song to listen to.

"For the record," Matt said in a bland voice, "I don't."

"Don't?"

"Say that . . . to all the girls. In case you were wondering." With that, he put his own earbuds in, leaving me wondering if there was a line we were crossing that I wasn't aware of.

I fell asleep with the memory of his skin on mine.

And for the first time in a year.

When I closed my eyes, I did it with a smile on my face.

Chapter Fifteen

MATT

I judged men who watched women sleep.

It was a thing.

A line you didn't cross.

I never found it romantic in movies, and I didn't find it romantic now. That wasn't why I was doing it. I wasn't hoping she'd wake up and go, *How long have you been staring?* If anything, she'd grab her shoe from her foot and hit me over the head with it repeatedly until I apologized and handed her a testicle on a silver platter.

No, I watched her out of the corner of my eye because she'd looked so peaceful, because a selfish part of me wanted to know what put that smile on her face, and the competitive part of me needed to know what it took to keep it there.

The plane landed too soon.

I stopped staring.

The smile was gone.

And I felt its loss like someone had just taken away a few extra beats of my heart and refused to give them back.

A town car was waiting for us after we grabbed our luggage, and the closer we got to the hotel, the more Parker fidgeted with the bangles on her wrists or the short fingernails she was hell-bent on destroying.

With a sigh, I finally grabbed her right hand. "You may need your fingers later."

"Huh?"

"You're chewing your nails down to nubs. I'm aware there's a very serious no-hands rule in soccer, but you may need them to catch all those tacos in the wild later."

She just exhaled and looked out the window. "Yeah, good point."

"Nervous?" Why the hell wasn't I moving my hand?

Furthermore, why was she letting me touch her? When days ago confronting her had her eyes bugging out of her head and her claws directed at my dick and everything else my body held dear?

"Dunno," she said.

Her hand became clammy, and then she dug her left hand into her mouth. I cleared my throat.

With an eye roll, she sat on it. "Better?"

I snorted out a laugh. "Thought only toddlers sat on their hands."

"You would know," she said sweetly without making eye contact.

"You're afraid," I whispered.

"I'd rather be angry."

A peculiar answer. One born out of knowing fear, facing its ugliness and deciding that to go down fighting and screaming, biting and cursing, was better than rocking in the corner and letting defeat take hold.

Way in over your head, Matt.

I almost chuckled.

Leave it to Willow to drop this one on my doorstep.

Damn it, Willow.

"What are you wearing tonight?" I changed the subject so that she would stop focusing on her fear and her need to lash out in order to send it packing. "A dress?"

"Masking tape and Sharpie." She flashed me a smart-ass grin. "You want first dibs on doodling?"

"I wouldn't trust me with a marker where you're concerned." I smirked.

Her eyes narrowed. "With my luck you'd draw penises all over me in full middle school humor."

"I was thinking something along the lines of tits, but yeah, that works too."

"Why draw what I already have?" she asked sweetly, causing me to flash a look at her chest and then look away. "Caught ya."

"I'm a guy. You say *tits*, I look. It's biology." I tugged at the collar of my shirt and then cleared my throat. "Seriously, though, what did you bring? Are you confident about your outfit?"

Silence. Followed by a noncommittal shrug.

"Right." I leaned toward the driver. "We need to stop off at the nearest department store, Saks, Barney's, Nordstrom—whatever's closest."

"Nordstrom is a block from your hotel."

"Perfect. You'll wait for us." I handed him a crisp hundred-dollar bill. "Keep the car running."

"Sir, yes, sir."

When I leaned back into my leather seat, Parker was giving me a confused look.

"What?" Suddenly feeling insecure, I dropped her hand and faced her. For some reason holding her hand made me uncomfortable, out of control, and I didn't like submitting control to someone so chaotic. Even though it was one of the things I loved about her most.

Shit, I was completely losing it.

"Nothing." She eyed me up and down. "Never mind."

"You can't give me a look like—" I frowned. "Wait, are you blushing?"

"Of course not!" she scoffed with a weak laugh as her cheeks reddened even more, and then she was running her palms down her white Nike joggers.

"You are." I leaned in and touched her right cheek with my fingertip. It was like I couldn't stop touching and provoking her. Maybe I liked the smiles, the blushes. Maybe I liked the yelling and the fighting. Maybe I wanted all of it in one chaotic, hurricane-filled package.

She shrugged away from my touch and was practically koala-hugging her door when she gave me an irritated look and said, "I was just going to say that was hot, what you just did, and now my embarrassment is complete, so if you could just give the nice man another Benjamin Franklin, I'll let him run me over with this nice, heavy piece of machinery."

I tried to hide my smile and ended up failing as I let out a low chuckle that made me feel lighter than I'd felt in years. "That may have been hot, but you, right now . . ." I shouldn't say it. I couldn't not say it. "Are adorable."

She scrunched up her nose. "Like a pet?"

"One I want to keep." I shrugged. "Not the kind you drop off at the farm, so consider yourself safe."

"You and your compliments, my head may explode." At least she was smiling at me, and I was smiling back in a moment I wanted to put on repeat again and again. The car pulled to a stop; too soon she looked away, giving me no reason to keep staring like an idiot.

"Mr. Kingston," our driver said politely.

"Thank you." I nodded as he hurried out of the car and opened Parker's door and then ran around and opened mine. I hated waiting, but it was part of his job, and I knew it was insulting not to. "We won't be long."

"Take your time, Mr. Kingston." He tipped his hat, revealing round spectacles and an easy yet aged smile and tanned face. "I brought my Kindle."

"Good man." I chuckled and then put my hand on Parker's back as we walked into the department store. I could tell she was trying to hide her shock because she had her unimpressed face glued on, but I could sense her excitement over the chic décor and expensive clothes. Hell, I could almost feel her body buzzing with it when we walked by all the salon shoes.

"This way." We went up three levels until we came to the personal shopper area. A woman in her midtwenties approached, wearing head-to-toe black with heels my sister would commit murder for. She had auburn hair and bright-blue eyes. "Do you have an appointment?"

"No." I smiled. "But I'll make it worth your while to fit us in. Shouldn't take more than ten minutes."

Her eyes narrowed in on me. "Do I know you?"

"I doubt it, just one of those faces."

Next to me, Parker rolled her eyes. I pinched her side, reminding her to behave. Money didn't get you everywhere, but it got you most places, and attitude was everything.

"Right." The woman rubbed her hands together. "I'm LaLa."

Parker pressed her lips together. Shit, she better not laugh.

LaLa eyed Parker up and down then shot me a confused look. "What exactly are you looking for?"

"A dress," I said simply. "White, something professional yet still sexy, alluring but not too much, and show off her curves. If you don't have white, stick with a solid color, no nylons. She'll need an open-toe boot that she can walk in."

"Done."

"Done?" Parker squealed. "What do you mean *done*?"

"I mean I have the perfect dress for your occasion. It's Versace, has capped sleeves, which should complement your muscle tone well. It's off-white, has crystals, and has been on preorder, but we just got our first shipment in this morning. If you're willing to pay the price."

"Sounds perfect," I said. "May we see it?"

Less than three minutes later, I was in the dressing room with a shaking Parker. The sales lady had made the mistake of letting her see the price tag, and since the dress was over four grand, she was having a moment. I should have had Willow do this, not that we'd had time between practices.

"Look." I put my hands on her shoulders. "You won't break it. The dress is beautiful, but you wear the dress, not the other way around."

Parker made a face in the mirror.

"I sound like a jackass, got it. I'll just be waiting out here."

"Wait!" Parker moved from one Converse to the other. "I know this is highly inappropriate, but I'm petrified I'm going to rip something and that haughty woman with the obviously fake name is going to say something like 'Told you so,' so could you just . . . help me, you know, with your eyes closed?"

I laughed. "You're better off on your own, you know that, right?"

"Please?"

It was the *please* that did me in, followed by the bottom-lip bite, and the innocent flick of her eyes as she waited for my answer.

I sighed, scratching the back of my head, blowing out a frustrated breath, and doing a semicircle like a trapped animal. "Fine, just not a word to anyone. Seriously . . . anyone." I pointed at her like she was a child.

Which got me an equally childish response: a Parker eye roll.

"Take your pants off, smart-ass," I grumbled, causing her to falter a bit as she kicked off her shoes and pulled off her joggers.

I didn't expect her to be wearing white, lacy boy shorts, but there they were, like a giant sign saying open, open, open.

I cleared my throat and unzipped the dress while she rustled with her shirt next to me. We somehow managed to turn at the same time.

I opened my mouth, closed it. "Not a word, Parker." It came out as a rasp, like I didn't mean it, quiet like I didn't want her to hear.

She squeezed her eyes shut and nodded like she was ashamed I had to even say it, like I'd said the wrong thing.

With shaking hands, she grabbed the dress from me and slowly stepped in. It fit her like a glove as I pulled it up and zipped all the way to the neck.

LaLa had great taste.

I wasn't sure how long I stared at Parker in the mirror. Sans makeup, with her hair in a ponytail, she outshone even the prettiest model I'd ever partied with.

"Better?" I managed to get out as she stared at herself in the mirror, a look of shock on her face.

She nodded just as my cell rang.

"Yelloooo!" Willow yelled in my ear.

I pulled it away and winced. "We need to work on your phone skills. What do you need?"

"So the team had to move the dinner up. I said you guys could meet at the hotel bar in a half hour."

"A half hour?" I repeated. "That's cutting it kind of close, but we can manage." I was already dressed in slacks and a dress shirt, my typical uniform when I wasn't training with Parker. "We can make it, we just need shoes."

"Shoes?" Willow said like a kid who'd just heard the word *candy*. "Why do you need shoes? Are you shopping without me?"

"Er . . . no." I gave Parker a panicked look while she burst out laughing. "Shit."

"DAMN YOU, MATT KINGSTON! YOU DON'T SHOP WITHOUT ME, EVER! We made a pact!"

"I was seven and you were a monster!"

"Whatever. What's she wearing? Wait, did you buy her a dress? Maaaatt? Hello? Matt?"

Was I staring at Parker again? Shit, I needed to focus.

"Yeah, what?"

"You're shopping."

"It's a possibility."

Chapter Sixteen

I wanted to hold his hand.

But I would die before admitting it.

I was wearing a dress that made me feel like a princess—powerful, confident, renewed. I would never confess it to anyone, least of all the man who made me feel worthy of wearing it, when I'd been a mess on the inside for so long.

A barrage of thoughts struck me when I saw the way he looked at me in the dress, the biggest one being that this could be more than a fresh start for my career. It could be a fresh start for everything. He looked at me like I belonged next to him, in this world, and for the first time in months I had hope. I could kiss him for giving me that opportunity, I would marry him in this dress and never look back.

And that's when I realized I was slowly pulling down the walls I'd erected and succumbing to Matt Kingston and his smiles, the way his eyes crinkled, the way he touched me like he was afraid I would break.

Or maybe afraid he would too.

The shoes were perfect, I'd never worn Valentino before; they were nude with a kitten heel, and were studded, which made me feel like a rock star. All in all, they were too expensive for me to purchase on my own, but if I had the money they would one hundred percent be what I would pick out for myself.

I kept staring at them as we walked, which meant he basically had to carry me into the lobby.

My feet didn't feel huge and awkward, and as our nice driver took our bags in to the bellhop, I looked down one last time and smiled.

"Matt Kingston." Matt gave his name to the restaurant host.

"Lovely," the woman said, beaming. "Your companions are already here, shall I take you?"

"Wait!" I blurted, grabbing Matt's elbow, holding us both in place.

"I'll just give you a minute." She winked.

"What if I yell at someone?" I wondered out loud, my eyes searching his, begging for some of his confidence to trickle down through our connection and give me strength. "What if I spill my water? What if—"

"Stop," he said a bit harshly. I almost backed up. And then he said, "If you yell, I'll yell too. I'll make them think that we can't hear them. If you spill your water, I'll just have to spill my wine—the point is, you don't walk in there by yourself, you walk in there with me."

"My agent." I nodded. "My coach."

His face hardened a bit. "Your friend."

And then he offered me his elbow.

I knew it would be wrong to ask for his hand.

But I wanted it. Needed it.

However, I knew they'd get the wrong idea.

I hated that people cared about things they had no business caring about. But I took the olive branch, the peace he offered, and placed my hand on his elbow. I held my head high. I'd put on some powder and mascara in the car, added a deep red to my lips, and called it good.

I knew how to do makeup, I just didn't see the point when I would sweat it all off.

I took another deep breath as we weaved through table after table until we reached a back booth. It was near the kitchen and seemed to be private, which was good. Private was good.

I smiled as one of the men turned. He had silver hair and a mustache that was still dark. His smile was friendly, and he was wearing an LA Rams baseball cap.

I immediately relaxed.

"Parker!" He held out his hands. I took them and leaned in as he kissed me on the cheek.

I liked him.

He seemed relaxed.

And he was wearing black jeans and a T-shirt instead of a stuffy suit. I kept imagining my old coach in these situations—pinstriped suits, expensive shoes, cologne, the whole stupid package.

But this guy? He seemed comfortable in his own skin. Yeah, I really liked him.

"Matt." He shook his hand. "Sorry for such short notice, but your assistant said you had already landed. I didn't realize my new assistant coach would be able to make the meeting, but his plane just landed as well."

"Wow, I didn't know you were looking to hire on." Matt shrugged and offered his hand to the other man with slicked-back dark hair. His back was still to us, and then he stood and turned.

I stumbled backward, partially hiding my body behind Matt.

"It's a pleasure to meet you." Erik held out his massive hand to Matt. I could see when Matt put two and two together because he squeezed Erik's hand longer than necessary while I forced a watery smile.

"I think I'll just use the restroom really quick," I said lamely, trying my best not to black out as I made my way toward the bathrooms on other side of the restaurant.

I shoved my way inside the women's restroom and braced my hands against the countertop as nightmares assaulted me.

"Stop saying no, Parker." He kissed my neck. "Nobody else does . . . Just think of where I could take your career."

"No." I shoved against him. "I can't, I'm not like that."

"Yeah, you are . . ." He gripped my ass as his length pressed against my body in a predatory way that confused me, made me feel wanted but wrong about the situation. I'd always idolized him. "I see the way you look at me, the way you want me."

"No." Did I? Did I look at him that way? Did I do something wrong? He was fun, and I'd always loved my coach and would have done anything for him.

He reached under my shirt and cupped my breasts. "Come on, Parker, we both want this, you know we do."

I ran into the stall and dry heaved, careful not to get anything on my pretty dress.

I stared at myself in the mirror. Don't be that girl anymore. You're not that girl anymore.

I fixed my hair. At least I could be calm on the outside while I freaked out on the inside. Maybe I could send Matt a quick text that I needed to leave early. It was just dinner and drinks. Anger surged through me, I knew better, dinner and drinks? If I blew them off I could ruin other offers. Erik must have known that too, otherwise he wouldn't have risked it. A sickness washed over me again, like he had his hands all over me, like he was doing it in front of Matt and showing Matt how easy I was when I knew I wasn't.

Why the hell was he even here?

He was supposed to be far, far away!

At my old school!

Not here!

Was he the one that suggested the interview?

The more I thought about it, the sicker I got.

I shoved the door open just in time to see Erik leave the men's restroom.

I quickly walked down the hall but felt him behind me every step of the way, and when he reached for my wrist, I jerked away, wanting to slam him into the nearest table.

Polite.

I had to be polite.

Tears stung the backs of my eyes.

Why was it impossible to be polite in a world full of monsters who looked like they just walked off a magazine cover?

"What?" I pasted a smile on my face. "Did you need more toilet paper?"

He narrowed his eyes. "Something between you and Kingston?"

"My agent?" My eyebrows shot up. "Why would you think that?"

"He's training you, he doesn't train his athletes, not typically, and he watches you."

"Everyone watches me," I said in a sarcastic, angry voice. "'Cause I'm so pretty."

"Still such a sarcastic bitch, I think that's what I missed most . . ." He leered at me in my dress. "Nice of him to get you all pretty for us. I bet he got you ready in the way only a man like Matt Kingston can. Why is it that you'd sleep with him to get ahead and yet with me—"

"Everything okay here?" Matt saved me, saved the entire day as well as Erik's life by showing up.

"Ah, just catching up. She was one of my favorite players, you know." Erik grinned dumbly.

"Right." Matt scratched the back of his head. "I punched my favorite coaches too, it's an athlete thing, but you wouldn't really know, though, since you were in the league, what, a day?"

I almost choked on a laugh at Erik's purple face. "Listen, Kingston—"

"We actually have two other meetings to get to," Matt interrupted. "So we should get back to the table before you get fired from another job, hmm, Erik?"

"I wasn't fired."

"Yeah, alright, our secret." Matt winked as he led me back to the table. I sat as close to him as humanly possible and dug into the bread basket to keep myself from yelling at Erik or throwing my nearest utensil.

The other coach, who I found out was named Billy and had five grandsons, gave me another warm smile. "So, the rumor mill is filled again with talks about you, my dear. Your talent is of course incredible, and I've even heard from your old coach here that the whole fight incident was blown out of proportion, and now that I've met you, I can only agree that you aren't that sort of person. You're refreshing, and the stats don't lie."

No, but humans did.

Men did.

I felt myself sway a bit.

And that's when Matt put his hand on my thigh and clenched it tight. Had I not known him, trained with him, trusted him, I would have lashed out. Instead, I put my hand on his and kept it there.

My anchor.

My escape.

My peace.

"Thank you, that's so sweet," I found myself saying. "The Seattle air has been good for me, that and just leaving a bad situation at my old school. I'm sure there are details I can fill you in on." I leveled Erik with a glare, but all it took was a smirk from him to bat down any bravery I had found, making me want to crawl under the table in a defeated puddle.

Matt spoke up. "She's been a wonder to teach, scored a couple goals on me, and I have her training with Jagger and Slade next week."

He did?

"You do?" Erik blurted.

"I figured why not train with the best if you want to be with the best team. And I have to be honest with you guys, we've gotten a lot of interest and it's still early. Her heart is in Seattle but we may be tempted by a sweeter offer."

Erik stared at us like he was trying to figure out if we were bluffing.

Billy stood. "Well, I think that's that. We'll stay in touch. Not sure if we can beat Seattle's offer, but I like to give second chances and I love some raw talent."

Second chances? It wasn't a second chance if you never got a first. Matt started rubbing my thigh.

"Thank you." I didn't stand, I felt paralyzed.

Erik stood just before Matt did, his eyes on our side of the table. I didn't drop my hand in time, although Matt jerked away fast enough.

Was I overthinking it?

Would he say something?

Why was he in a position to ruin my life again?

I scooted out after Matt and shook Billy's hand and begrudgingly did the same to Erik, only he refused to give it back right away.

No, he had to kiss the back of my hand, linger over it, and then whisper, "It's wonderful to see you again, little all-star."

I almost puked in my mouth. "Y-you too."

They left amidst more handshakes while I followed behind Matt. After they left the hotel, Matt turned to me, anger in his eyes.

"Matt, I can ex—"

He put his fingers up then motioned to the bartender. "I'm going to need bottles of Skyy, Hennessy, mixers, and what the hell, toss in some Tanqueray." He slid the bartender two Franklins. "Charge it to our room, it's under Kingston."

"Number?"

Matt pulled out his keycard. "Penthouse suite 10021."

"Right away, sir." The bartender took the money, and Matt took my hand.

"Should I check into my room?"

Matt stopped walking, looked at me, then grabbed his phone and dialed. "Willow, the penthouse suite, I'm assuming it has a connecting door to Parker's room?"

Silence.

More tangible anger on his end.

In fact, his face was turning a nice shade of Will Kill Willow Later red.

"Fine," he barked, and then I was getting tugged toward the elevators.

With shaking hands, he slid the keycard in and hit the top-floor button.

"I know you're angry," I whispered with tears in my eyes. "At me. I don't even know what you're thinking, except—"

Matt hit the stop on the elevator, scaring the shit out of me. "Did he touch you?"

I nodded.

Matt braced my shoulders with his hands. "Did he hurt you?"

Another nod as a tear slid down my face, kissing my mouth.

And finally, the question I knew would follow. "Is that why you punched him on national television?"

I burst into tears.

All over his nice shirt.

All over my pretty dress.

In a hanging death trap, almost twenty floors up.

And he held me.

He held me against him and let me cry.

I didn't realize we were moving again until the doors opened to a beautiful hallway with one door.

He slid the card again and helped me in.

I wiped my cheeks just as another knock sounded.

"God, that better be alcohol," Matt muttered under his breath as he opened the door and let in one of the wait staff.

They'd basically brought him an entire bar, even more than what he requested.

Matt tipped him.

The waiter left.

And silence fell again.

I was afraid to look anywhere but Matt's face, afraid I'd miss something, maybe even afraid that I'd miss the disappointment that I needed to see in order to stop falling for him like I knew I was.

I needed the rejection so it wouldn't hurt when he stopped touching the back of my hand to make sure I was alright, or kissing my cheek just because.

His back was turned to me as he started filling cups with ice. "Have you taken any anxiety meds in the last twenty-four hours?"

"No," I choked out.

"Good." He shoved a drink in my face, unbuttoned his shirt a few buttons, sat next to me on the fancy barstool, and said in a low voice, "Tell me everything."

Chapter Seventeen

Everything?

I gulped down half my drink. "Where do you want me to start?"

"At the beginning, where most stories typically start. I think I already know how things ended . . ."

"Things." I snorted and looked down at my shaking hands. Matt took the drink from me and grabbed them, encompassing them with his warmth as he scooted his barstool closer.

The hotel room was filled with that static silence that buzzed around a person's ears and made them want to shiver a bit with the emptiness. I choked back a sob as I finally met Matt's eyes and started my story. "Everyone loved him, the coaching staff respected him, my teammates all but worshipped him. We always used to joke about how hot he was." I shuddered. "Lots of the girls even said they'd paid for private training, which just made us roll our eyes, but it was all speculation. He was a flirt and charismatic."

"He's a douche," Matt said in a cold voice.

"Yeah." My voice cracked. "He's that too."

Silence descended again as Matt waited for me to say more, but I'd rather have hurled myself from the penthouse window. I didn't want

Matt to look at me with disappointment, not after all of the pride I'd seen in his eyes.

Somehow, I again felt Erik's eyes on my skin, his lingering peppermint breath as he tried to kiss his way down my neck. I reached for my drink again then rested my hand on Matt's. "It snowballed, that's the only way I can explain it. One day he was teasing me, accidentally touching me and apologizing for it, and I just didn't think anything of it, you know? I was a senior then. He'd never touched me before, but he started asking me to stay late after practice. It was when a lot of teams got interested, so he said I needed to put in twice the amount of work."

I couldn't look at Matt's face, but I felt his heavy breathing, his anger as it swarmed between us, ready to strike out at any time.

I exhaled. "It was late, the trainer had left, and Erik said I needed to make sure that I stretched, so he told me to lie down on the table. When I did he joked about me being too sweaty and said to take off my shirt since I was still in a sports bra. It made sense, I was drenched and uncomfortable." I could still smell the antiseptic in the air, see the yellow lights as they flickered overhead as I lay back, and I winced. "He started stretching my legs, nothing unusual, but his hands moved higher and higher until I kind of, I don't know, flinched against him." Nausea rolled in my stomach. "He held my legs down and then laughed when I struggled. I jumped down and finally pulled away from him as he backed me against the wall. He said I should stop saying no, that nobody else ever did. And then he said he could help my career." I hung my head in shame. "And a part of me was afraid that he was right. That he could make or break me. I shoved him away, told him I wasn't like that." Tears welled in my eyes. "And you know what his answer was?"

Matt's grip on my hands tightened. "That I was. He said I *was* like that as he gripped my ass, and then I felt—" Matt bit out a curse. "I felt him against me . . . completely aroused. I hated myself in that moment because a part of me wanted to have his attention when everyone else wanted it, but it was fleeting." I paused. "He said I looked at him a certain way, and I wondered if I did something wrong. Was it because I wore my hair down and he yelled at me to put it up? Was it because my shorts were too short? Did I lead him on or do something wrong? And then he slid his hands under my bra and told me I wanted him. I was so damn confused, so when he kissed me . . ." It felt like someone had punched me in the stomach. "When he kissed me, I kissed him back—briefly—and then he started undressing me more." Matt leaned toward me like he was ready to either pull me in for a hug or reach for more alcohol. "And the worst part is, mentally I was fighting him, I was telling myself it was wrong, but I was afraid that if I didn't give him what he wanted, he'd ruin my career. I realized then that he'd probably done it to other girls, but at the time I just thought that they'd had disrespectful attitudes." I reached for my drink again. "It was over fast." I downed its contents. "I don't know what I expected, not what he said . . ."

"What did he say?" Matt's voice was low, dangerous, predatory.

I finally looked up into Matt's furious gaze. "He said he thought it would take longer to break me and laughed at how easy it was—how easy I was." Tears spilled over my cheeks. "And then he left me alone with all the evidence of what we'd done still on my body. He shut the door. And the next day I was called into the assistant director's office for behavior issues with my coach and sent to therapy. I found out later that he was sleeping with the therapist and three other girls from the team, and when I approached the AD about it weeks later I was too late, he'd beaten me to it. Erik made up stories about how I'd been sending him love letters, how I was obsessed with him, how I got angry when I didn't get my way."

"That fucking bastard!" Matt rose to his feet. "Why didn't you tell me?"

"Why didn't I tell you?" My eyebrows shot up. "Are you serious? Since when has anyone ever been on my side? Believed me? Plus, it's not like I could go to anyone and say it wasn't consensual, because it was! I still did it! I still let him—" I looked down at my shaking hands. "I still let him touch me, take advantage of me, see? It's better to be angry. Fear only makes you do stupid things you can't come back from. At least anger gives you the power back."

Matt hung his head and grabbed my glass, filled it up again, handed it back, and asked, "Is there more?"

I snorted. "Oh yeah, the jackass pursued me the rest of the season . . . constantly cornering me, taunting me. I rejected him every time. I talked to the AD again and one of the girls from my team, but they believed him over me. He'd poisoned the well, and whenever people saw us together they assumed the worst, that I'd done the cornering, the seducing. And the morning of the championships, he—" I hugged my arms around my waist and tried to tuck myself away from the world.

Matt chugged his drink and pulled me into his embrace, surrounding me in his protective warmth, rocking me back and forth as my teeth started to chatter.

"It was raining," I whispered against his chest. "I ran back into the locker room, the game wouldn't start for another two hours. He was waiting. He pulled me into his office, called me a cunt and numerous other things. I stood there and took it, asked to leave, and he—he hit me when I refused to have sex with him."

"He hit you?" Matt's voice was so on edge I wasn't sure if I was safer out of his arms or in them.

"Yeah. He tried to pull my shorts down, I kicked him in the shin, ran out of the locker room with him chasing me literally onto the field, and when he called me a slut in front of the entire team, I lost it. I just . . . punched him. I didn't care who saw, didn't care that it would ruin my entire life, because in that moment all that mattered was that he'd feel the same embarrassment and pain he'd caused me. The media was already camped out, they saw it all."

Matt rocked me back and forth. He ran his hands over my hair, and then he said something I had no idea I needed to hear until that moment.

"I believe you."

Chapter Eighteen

Matt

She sagged in my arms like she'd been carrying the weight of the world on her shoulders, and I felt like the biggest dick in the universe for not seeing it sooner.

The way she hated being backed into a corner.

Her fear of darkness.

The way she lashed out.

Her behavior toward men in general.

I should have seen all of it.

From her attitude to the way she carried herself, I should have known. I was better at my job than that, not that I was trained to notice those sorts of things, but I'd still like to think I should be better. I'd let my own anger at my attraction turn me into someone I didn't even recognize.

And now I just felt guilt and a hell of a lot of shame that I'd possibly made her feel even worse about herself when all I wanted was to take all the pain and humiliation away.

"I feel guilty for not telling Willow," she said against my chest, her breath warm, her body hanging on mine like she couldn't stand on her own two feet even if she tried.

"Why haven't you told her?"

"Talking about it makes it real," she whispered in a hoarse voice. "I just . . . I hate him so much, I hate him."

"Want me to send a guy after him? I'm sure we could make it look like an accident." Her lips twitched while she wiped away another tear. "Think about it, we make it look like an accident, superglue his dick to his hand, turn on the puppy channel, and then pump his drink full of Viagra. Nothing worse than when a pug does it for you . . ."

Parker burst out laughing against my chest. "Sounds like a plan, I'll ride shotgun."

"Attagirl." I hugged her tighter. "You aren't the only victim in this, Parker . . . just think about what that means . . . and know that as your agent I'll stand behind you no matter what you decide, but as your friend I encourage you to go to the proper authorities, because he's just going to keep doing it until he gets caught. He's a narcissist through and through."

"I still . . ." She pulled away and looked up at me, a mixture of hope and worry in her eyes. "I still let him," she said, her voice cracking.

"I'm going to ask you something, and no matter what your answer is, know there isn't any judgment, alright?"

She nodded.

"Would you have let him had he just come on to you and not mentioned your career? Making or breaking you?"

"No." She said it quickly and then slumped forward, her forehead resting against my chest. "I'm a horrible person."

"No!" I gripped her by the shoulders. "You're not a horrible person. You were put in a shitty situation with someone who abused his authority. That's not on you, that's on him."

"I wish I believed that," she said with a watery smile.

"Give it time." I wiped the tears from her cheeks with my thumbs. "And until then, we drink."

"Matt Kingston encouraging alcohol consumption during training?" She laughed through more tears. "What happened to you?"

"Parker Speedman," I said simply, as if she should know she was the driving force behind a lot of my behavior lately. The sad part was that I knew in that moment, I would never act on any of my feelings, no matter how deep they went. I would die keeping them to myself.

Because the last thing she needed was another man in her life to let her down.

"*Deadpool 2* sound good?" I grabbed the remote while she started refilling our drinks.

"That's it, huh? You're not pissed? Shocked? Angry?"

"I'm all of those things, but none of them are directed at you." I stared at the remote for a few brief seconds as I felt her walk toward me. She set the drinks on the table.

Our eyes locked.

I saw disappointment there.

I felt it in my own gaze too. We both knew that the invisible line we'd been dancing around was firmly back in place because right now she needed the professional relationship more than she would ever admit.

And that's all I could be for her.

I gave her a sad smile and then sat on the cushy leather couch and grabbed one of the blankets provided by the hotel.

She sat down next to me.

We enjoyed our drinks.

We laughed.

And when she began to drift to sleep against my shoulder, I squeezed my eyes shut and forced myself to stay in control. "Parker . . ."

"Hmm?" Her eyes flickered open. "What time is it?"

"Past midnight," I murmured with a smile. "We should go to bed." Separate beds.

"Okay." She frowned up at me and looked around. "Is mine through some weird hidden door or something?"

"Bedroom." I pointed to the opposite end of the penthouse. "I'm taking the couch."

"Wait, why are you on the couch?" Her heavily lidded gaze was slowly killing me inside, right along with her swollen lips and puffy cheeks. She was beautiful, so beautiful . . . My fingers trembled with the need to reach out and cup her face, trace her chin, kiss down her neck.

"Because apparently the hotel was at capacity, so Willow only booked us one room," I grumbled. "You need a good night's sleep. Let me take the male species' punishment tonight and wake up with a pain in my neck." I flashed a grin. "I don't mind, go relax. At least we have two bathrooms."

"God forbid we have to share and you find a hair by your toothbrush again," she said with a smirk.

"Very funny." I glared playfully, and before I realized what I was doing, I reached out and twisted her hair around my finger.

I swallowed slowly and looked away as the sound of our joint breathing filled the room.

"Thanks, Matt." Her voice was quiet, trusting. Damn it. Keep it under control!

"Not all men are like him," I said as I stood and helped her to her feet.

"I know." Her eyes locked onto me so hard I couldn't look away. "And you promise you're not mad?"

I sighed. "I don't know whether to lock you up away from men like him, or kiss you and prove that we aren't all monsters."

Parker's eyes widened a bit.

"Night," I said firmly, struggling to hold onto my resolve.

"Good night," she parroted and slowly backed away then turned and walked toward the hall.

I watched her go, then I grabbed my suitcase and wheeled it toward the other bathroom. I stripped down into pajama pants and brushed my teeth, then flicked off the lights and made my way back to the lonely couch with the TV's light casting a glow across where I'd spend my night.

Without her.

Why the hell was I fixating on what I couldn't have?

"Hey, Matt?" Her voice was going to slowly kill me, wasn't it? Burn me from the inside out, taunt me with everything that was off-limits for a very severe reason.

"Yeah?" My voice was gravelly, aroused. Perfect. Fucking perfect. She could probably hear the strain.

She made her way down the hall, hair hanging past her shoulders, tank top showing off a bit of midriff, and my eyes drank in her short red shorts, hips, and muscular thighs. I wheezed out an exhale.

"I forgot toothpaste." She made a face. "If I promise not to spit in it or put an eyelash on the cap and screw it back—can I borrow yours?" Her grimace widened into a grin.

I tossed a pillow at her. "Bathroom, and if I see any hair that's foreign, I'm waking you up every hour on the hour to do push-ups."

"Yeah, okay." She winked and breezed past me, smelling like flowers and a warm summer day.

I groaned into my hands, walked over to the little liquor cart, and poured a shot of whiskey.

"Got any more of that?" she asked behind me.

"Brave girl, taking a shot after toothpaste." I handed her a glass. "You should be in bed."

"Same goes for you." She took the shot and winced. "Yeah, that wasn't a good combo."

I took her glass and set it down. "No."

"I'm ready."

"For?" I smirked. "A bedtime story?"

"Wait, you have bedtime stories? Have you been holding out on me?"

"You'll never know." I jerked my head toward the hall. "Bedtime."

"Bedtime," she repeated, licking her lips.

I took a deep breath as she brushed past me, then curiosity got me. "What were you ready for?"

"Your kiss," she called over her shoulder with a confident smile.

"Bed." My voice shook.

She nodded her head once, defeat clouding her eyes.

I wiped my hands down my face as I watched her make her way down the hall, and then my feet were carrying me toward her and I was hauling her into my arms. Refusing to corner her in any dark hallway, I pulled her back into the living room. And there . . . I pressed my mouth against hers. She opened for me so perfectly that the ache in my chest worsened, needing more than I'd realized I needed. I parted her lips with my tongue and explored. She tasted of whiskey and toothpaste. She dug her fingers into my hair and then wrapped her arms around my neck as I pulled her against me. Seconds passed, I prayed for, wished for, more minutes, hours. Instead, I sucked on her lower lip, I memorized the feel of her body pressed against mine, I mourned the loss of it before she was even gone. And I gently pried myself away. And because I couldn't help it, I kissed her cheek, and then I trailed down her neck with kisses and whispered, "Real men don't force a woman."

"No." She rose up on her tiptoes and brushed a soft kiss across my lips. "Real men kiss like that."

I almost grabbed her wrist.

I almost tugged her against me and begged her to let me into her room.

There were so many *almosts* that hung in the balance between right and wrong.

So I let her go.

I watched the sway of her hips as she walked off.

And I sent a fucking text to Slade when I couldn't fall asleep.

Me: I'm fucked.

Slade: Yeah, you are.

Me: WTH? Why aren't you on my side?

Slade: We're talking about Parker, right? About the way Jagger says you watch her? About the only girl you've ever trained? Tread carefully, my friend.

Me: We kissed.

Slade: Uh . . .

Me: Never mind. Can you put together a night out for everyone this next weekend when training's over for her? A celebration of sorts?

Slade: No, but Mack would love to. You know how she is.

I smiled down at my phone. Yeah, his wife was one of my favorite people. I liked her even more than Slade, and that was saying a lot— the guy was my best friend.

Slade: Crying into a bottle of wine yet? Breaking shit?

Me: Not yet.

Slade: Hah, yeah give it time.

Me: That wasn't at all helpful.

Slade: Get some sleep, you'll need it.

I set my phone down and then stared at the blank screen and wondered how I was even going to treat her normally without wanting more from her.

Yeah, the next week of training was going to be a nightmare, wasn't it?

Chapter Nineteen

PARKER

I spent the flight trying not to steal glances at Matt while he worked on his computer. And then I spent even more time dissecting every little thing he did. Had the kiss been just to prove something? Was it more? Did it matter? I mean after confessing everything I'd confessed, I wouldn't touch me with a ten-foot pole—make that twenty.

But we'd kissed.

And it had made every other kiss I'd ever had seem like practice before the big game. His lips had been so soft, demanding, yet, ugh. I should not be thinking about his lips while I was sitting next to him.

My knee started bouncing nervously.

Matt's arm shot out and pressed it down.

I huffed. "Sorry."

"Something on your mind?" he asked, not looking up from the computer screen.

I glared.

"Saw that."

"You saw what?"

"You stuck your tongue out at me." The corners of his mouth lifted into an amused smile as he kept typing. Tap, tap, tap. With each tap of his fingers my irritation rose until I wanted to shake him and say something stupid like, DO YOU LIKE ME?

I mean of course he tolerated me.

If I was being completely honest, I hadn't expected him to respond to any sort of kiss from me, I had expected it to be a polite *Chin up*, or *There, there, not all men are monsters*.

Instead it was all passion, heat. It was something I wanted to explore; heck, I wanted to rip it open and bask in it.

And yet there he was, tapping away!

Our plane had been delayed, which meant we weren't getting home until later, which also meant I was a day behind in training, but the sleep would be welcome.

When Matt didn't say anything else, I put on my headphones, crossed my arms, and pretended to sleep. Mature, but I had no other option.

And then I did actually fall asleep because the plane landing jolted me forward. Matt grabbed my hand.

I tore off my headphones. "We're home? Already?"

His smile was bright, and might I even say a bit arrogant as he looked his fill. "Yeah, Cheetah Girl, we're home."

I shook my head at him. "Should have never told you that name."

"One day you may have to show me more of those moves."

"Think you could handle it? Maybe I'll rent you a cane just in case." I winked.

He glowered. "I'm not . . . old."

"Do you get a senior discount yet?"

"Do you want to walk home?"

I stared down at our still-joined hands. "Do you promise to hold my hand the whole way?"

He opened his mouth and shut it as I clung to him. And I smiled in womanly satisfaction when we exited the airplane.

Still holding hands.

◆ ◆ ◆

The house looked dark as Matt pulled the car into the open garage. I yawned behind my hand as he killed the engine. My legs felt like I'd done nothing but run all day, that's what travel always did to me. I wanted my own bed, a shower.

I froze.

Since when was the guest room my bed? Why did it feel more like home than any place I'd ever lived?

I frowned as Matt grabbed my duffel along with his bag and opened the door to the house for me.

"Thanks," I mumbled, not meeting his eyes as I walked in and flipped on the living room lights. "Oh, shit!"

Jagger stood there with nothing but a smile, and a pillow covering himself.

"What the hell!" Matt roared. "How do you even have a key? Did Willow let you in? Wait." Matt's jaw started ticking. "Where is Willow?"

"Baby, I'm ready for you!" Willow came bouncing into the room wearing nothing but black thigh-highs and a matching corset and clutching a can of whipped cream in her right hand. "Matt! I thought your flight was delayed?" She hid the whipped cream. I almost slapped my own face. Too late, bestie, too late.

"JAGGER!" Matt thundered. He was ready to charge like a bull. I quickly put myself in between both men. "OUT OF THE WAY, PARKER!"

I winced as he yelled over my head. "No! Just take a minute to think this through."

"Think what through!" And the vein was making an appearance. "He's naked in my house alone with my sister—and she has—" he sputtered. "Willow!"

"Stop yelling!" she yelled right back. "I'm an adult, and if you must know, I told him that the garbage disposal wasn't working."

I squeezed my eyes shut and tried not to laugh while Matt's chest heaved like he was storing all his energy so he could decapitate Jagger as soon as I moved out of the way.

"I fixed it," Jagger said in a cocky voice. "Just in case you were wondering."

Matt lunged.

"Whoa, whoa." I held him back. "Hey." I cupped his face with my hands without thinking. "Look at me, just look at me."

Matt's crazed expression met mine and immediately softened. "I'm killing them, pick who goes first."

I grinned. "You're not killing your only sister, and you're not killing one of your best players, plus he makes you good money, right?"

Jagger choked out a laugh. "Voice of reason."

"Not now, Jagger," Willow hissed.

"You're tired," I murmured to Matt in my best soothing voice. "Just go to bed and I'll talk to Willow. You can talk with Jagger in the morning."

He didn't move.

I hoped he'd listen. Then again, it was Matt, and he could do whatever he wanted; it was his house.

Oh no, what if he kicked her out? And me too?

Panic seized my lungs.

"Hey . . ." He tilted my chin up. "You okay?"

"Perfect," I lied through my fear and the tears that were building in my eyes at the thought of not seeing him again. "I just, I think I'm tired too."

"Ummmmm." Willow's voice broke through my thoughts and the lingering gaze I was giving Matt. Crap, he was still touching me. "Are we missing something?"

"Nothing you need to know," Matt said before letting me go and stepping away. I hated that he dropped his hands like he had no right to touch me in front of other people. I hated it so much I wanted to yell at him, to lash out. But I didn't. Maybe that was progress?

"Don't kill each other," was all I managed to say as I made my way toward my bedroom, the one in his house, the one he owned.

I changed for bed.

I stared up at the ceiling and wondered how I would survive the after.

After Matt.

After our friendship was over.

After I wasn't living in his house, under this roof.

After everything changed and I was on a team.

I was happy.

For the first time in a year.

Truly happy.

I didn't want that happiness ripped away.

And it occurred to me in a moment of frustration that soccer wasn't the only thing that completed me.

Apparently, my heart had room for more.

I just wished it was possible.

I turned over and sighed, I'd completely forgotten that I was blanketed in darkness. Maybe because it was his house, maybe because I was just so consumed with thoughts of his tenderness. Of his loyalty.

And just as I was about to reach for the lamp, my door cracked open. It was his face.

The one I knew I'd dream about when I closed my eyes.

He leaned over the bed.

I sucked in a breath as he brushed a kiss across my forehead. "Are you okay?"

I nodded because I knew if I said yes I'd cry or beg him to stay with me and kiss me again.

"I'm sorry I lost my head, I never want you to think that . . ." His voice lowered and cracked a bit. "I would never be angry enough to be violent, I just wanted you to know that. I would never physically hurt my sister—hurt you."

I exhaled and put a hand on his forearm. "I know."

Neither of us moved.

His fingers dug into the comforter like he was contemplating ripping it from the bed.

Awareness spread throughout my body as I watched his fingers twitch and flex. I wanted him to give in so badly.

"Parker—"

"MAAATT!" Willow's voice echoed down the hall. "I'm dressed now!"

He stood abruptly and turned on the lamp. "Dream happy dreams, Parker."

"Any suggestions?" I asked in a thick, lustful voice I recognized as my own.

He just shook his head and then winked, closing the door behind him.

Leaving my body with a hard buzz.

And my heart galloping in my chest.

Chapter Twenty

MATT

I went to bed aroused.

Woke up aroused.

Fucking drank my coffee watching the damn birds outside—aroused.

Took another cold shower and then hated myself when I wanted to relieve the aching sensation with visions of her mouth on my skin, her taste on my lips.

I suddenly saw prison in my future as I walked around with a perpetual hard-on. One day, I'd bump into an elderly lady, she'd try to whack it with a newspaper, and because it had been unappeased for so long, that would only encourage it more and well, there you go, national news, prison.

Death.

Dramatic. I was being dramatic, and Slade was no help whatsoever, from his laughter that morning when I'd called, to the emojis he'd been sending me since I went to my office.

It was going to be a long, hard day.

Hah.

Hard.

"Ready!" Parker came flying into my room in spandex shorts and a loose tank top, her hair pulled back in a braid and her skin looking—edible.

I choked on my cup of coffee. "G-great."

"You okay?" She put her hands on her hips. "Did you not sleep well?"

"You mean before or after I buried Willow's body out by the dead goldfish last night?" I rubbed my eyes with the back of my hands.

"Nice one." Parker pulled out a chair and put up her Nikes on my desk. Again.

I flicked them with my pencil. "Is this gonna be a thing?"

"At least my shoes are clean. I could have my cleats on, and leave little patches of sod all over your desk, maybe even a hair from the stadium for good measure."

I gagged. "You're a monster."

She smiled sweetly. "I'm what you made me, Coach."

Coach.

Agent.

Seventh circle of hell.

I mentally waved as Satan escorted me to my spot in the fiery middle.

I was here to be her supporter, I was not here to kiss the hell out of her and lock her in my room while making sweet love to her. It would be nice. More than nice, incredible. It was wrong.

Wrong.

Wrong.

Wrong.

I was all she had. I just needed to keep telling myself that.

Parker dropped her feet and leaned forward, resting her arms on her knees. "Are you sure you're okay?"

"Yeah." I sighed. "Just a long day. I think I need to run it off."

"Then let's do it."

Had I been drinking coffee I would have sputtered it all over my laptop and her face. She wanted to . . . exercise? Voluntarily? The woman who threatened me every day during training?

I leaned closer, felt her forehead with the back of my hand, only to get it slapped away. "You feeling okay?"

"Hey, I'm just trying to be a good client!"

And there it was again.

She looked so happy, so . . . free that I had to laugh and then wince when I realized that I could either sit there and lust after her or join her. "I could use a run."

"Remember, it's six and a half miles to the stadium. It can be our warm-up?" Her eyes were so hopeful, so adorable.

"Yeah." Just give me twenty minutes or a year for this to go down and I'll be right out. Why was my body betraying me? "I'll just go get dressed."

"Great." She stood like she was waiting.

"After . . . one last phone call." I cleared my throat.

"Oh." Hurt flashed in her expression before she stood. "Sure, I need to grab my ear pods anyways!"

She jogged out of my office while I pretended to pick up the phone. I finally calmed myself down enough to stand and make my way to my bedroom. I put on a pair of tight boxer briefs and my joggers, then grabbed a tank and my own pods.

She was already out in the living room stretching, and a smile broke out on her face when she saw me. "We racing?"

"Hah!" I wagged my finger at her. "Yeah no, we aren't racing for over six miles, not sure my old heart could take it."

She licked her lips. "Well, at least you have the body of an eighteen-year-old."

"Skinny and awkward?" I elbowed her. "Thanks."

She burst out laughing just as I jabbed my buds in and bolted out the door yelling behind me, "See you there!"

She sped past me; I caught up easily.

And even though we were both listening to music, we ran in perfect cadence, a perfect stride the entire way to the stadium. I was almost sad it was over, until she saw me grab my whistle and her face went from content to murderous.

"You brought that thing?"

"What?" I held the whistle out. "This?"

She tried to snatch it.

I backed up and ran onto the turf, holding it above my head. "What? Did the run not knock you out? Tell you what, if you can take the whistle from me, you can have it."

I'd never seen her look so competitive, so ready to rip me apart limb by limb.

And then I winked and blew it.

Bad idea.

She charged me.

I stumbled backward and ran, putting a bag of balls between us. She jumped them and came barreling toward me.

She jumped again, and I caught her midair then twisted her around as her body wiggled against mine, her ass bumping me in the best possible way.

I almost groaned when she finally broke free. Thank God for small miracles.

"Hand it over and I won't kick you in the junk," she teased with a smirk.

"Kick me in the junk and I guarantee I'll never father a child. Don't do that to a man." I tossed the whistle from hand to hand above her.

"I've got chops, old man."

"Oh yeah, Cheetah Girl?" I burst out laughing while she jumped in front of me and tried swiping it from my hand, it was so adorable that I grabbed her around the waist, tossed her over my shoulder, and ran toward the goal line.

"Maaaaatt!" she yelled, smacking my back, my ass, every piece of skin she could access.

"Gooooaaaallllllll!" I boomed once we reached the goal, and then I tossed her on her feet and ran around her in circles. "Ahhhh, and the crowd goes wild!"

She put her hands on her hips, laughing. "Matt Kingston, did you just score with me?"

And because I was too happy to lie and completely uncensored with that same happiness, I just shrugged and whispered, "I wish."

She didn't show any surprise or shock, just sauntered over to me like she was about to give me everything I wanted and needed in that moment. She wet her lips. God, I wanted to taste her. It was at the top of my bucket list and would be even after I did it.

A task I would never tire of.

Something that my heart and body would never consider completed.

A box that could have a million checks next to it and still have room for one more.

She leaned up on her tiptoes and brushed a soft kiss across my lips, then swiped the fucking whistle from my right hand and jumped up and down. "WINNER!"

I clapped. "Wow, good job, cheater."

"It's not cheating if you were planning on it anyway. That's what I like to call opportunity."

"Really?" I nodded. "Opportunity, huh?"

She kept dancing, so I tossed her back over my shoulder while she blew the whistle then dropped her on her ass next to the bag of balls. "Guess that means we're starting with burpees. We were going to start with drills, but someone stole my whistle." And my heart, and my everything. "I want thirty."

"I thought whoever held the whistle held the power, like the Ring but not near as flashy?" she grumbled as she started her first burpee.

141

"Power is always equal between us." I shrugged. "The whistle was just a reason to get you to fight back. If you lose your fight, you've lost the game."

She stopped doing her burpees, chest heaving. "You're too smart."

"Yeah." I stared her sweaty body down. "That's what I'm feeling now."

After ten, she pulled off her shirt.

And I was welcomed back into hell again.

Chapter Twenty-One

"I can't move my legs!" I yelled at Matt. We'd had two more days of training, and the guy had gotten more and more grumpy as the days went by. Sunday's practice had been so playful and fun.

Then Monday happened.

Willow warned me not to get in his way.

The man was like a bear who found out all the honey sources in the world had been completely depleted.

Like a vampire who didn't have his True Blood.

I even gave him back his whistle, wondering if his attitude was some weird thing about a girl beating him.

But he barely even said thank you.

And now?

Now I was kicking balls toward his face with glee.

He'd called me slow.

And then he asked if I was on my period because I was getting more tired than usual.

The nerve of the guy, I mean really.

I kicked a ball toward his junk and shrugged when he deflected it and shot me a glare. "Sorry."

"Was that necessary?"

"What crawled up your ass and died?" I fired back, kicking another ball. "You've been like this since Monday. It's Wednesday, and my tryouts are this Sunday. Could you try to be more . . . cheerful?"

"No," he said in a deadpan voice. "This"—he pointed to his face—"is all the cheer I have right now."

"Is it Willow?"

"No," he growled.

"Is it me?" I stopped kicking. "You can tell me if it's me, just tell me what I need to do, I can do better. Just—"

"Shut the hell up!" he roared. And then his face fell. "I'm sorry. I didn't mean that."

I put my hands up toward him.

He flinched. "It's not you, it's Erik."

I dropped my hands immediately. "Wh-what?"

"He's called me three times about you. The last message was to warn me against girls willing to spread their legs for opportunity, and just this morning there was a letter sent to the house with your name on it, no return address. It looked suspicious so I opened it, and inside was a picture of you with your college team with a heart drawn around your face."

The breath whooshed from my lungs, and I fell to the ground on my knees.

"I didn't delete the messages and I kept the letter," he admitted, walking over to me and putting an arm around my shoulders. "And you know I don't believe him. I already let the commissioner know what he was doing, and they're looking into it and his past behaviors to see if anyone else has come forward. And nothing. Nobody has said anything—"

"I'm not lying!" I yelled. Tears poured down my face, and when I swiped them from my cheeks, my hands came away wet and gritty with the dirt from practice.

"Parker, look at me." He gripped my chin. "I know that, don't you know I know that? This isn't about you. This is about the other girls who are silent. Because if he's bold enough to do this to you, he's bold enough to do it to others, and what makes you think he isn't threatening them? Isn't making them think that he can make or break them? And not just women your age, young girls too. I just found out Sunday night he taught an Olympic-development soccer camp last week. I can't . . . I can't imagine him at a camp with underage girls, it makes me want to vomit, and all they have is speculation, since I haven't mentioned your name other than the threatening messages . . ."

My hands shook as I stared down at them. "My greatest fear is saying something and having everyone call me a slut just like he did."

"They may do just that," he said. "But you have to ask yourself if it's worth it. Is it worth it—if you save one girl? If you save two?"

"MATT!" Slade's voice carried across the stadium. I jumped a foot as Matt cursed under his breath and turned to the two approaching forms. I'd forgotten they were going to practice with us later today.

Jagger and Slade, two of the best male soccer athletes in the world. Both infamous playboys, although Jagger was clearly still in that category while Slade was happily married and, according to Matt, trying for baby number one.

They dropped their duffels on the sidelines and peeled off their shirts.

"Apparently they're skins?" I offered lamely.

Matt put his hand on my shoulder. "Do you want to do this another time?"

"Nope. We're training, so let's train. We can talk about this later?"

He nodded.

He also looked disappointed in me, but he didn't know what it was like to be pushed so far, to be told that everything you had to offer the world had to do with what you could offer one man.

I stood, wiped the dirt from my cheeks, and flashed the guys a smile. "Ready to lose?"

"Ah, I see she hasn't lost her arrogance." Slade winked and then shared a knowing look with Matt.

Something passed between them, something that seemed like it was about me, and my chest felt a bit heavy.

Did Slade know about the kiss?

Did Jagger?

As if I had summoned him, Jagger walked by and mussed my hair. "Aw, now you look like you've been playing hard. Alright, kiddo, let's do this."

"I'm not your kiddo," I fired back. "Plus Willow, you know her, right? The one who got naked and—"

"Son of a bitch." Jagger looked up at the sky. "Nothing happened, Matt, I swear."

"Yet," Slade coughed.

"I'm uninviting you for Christmas." Jagger glared at him.

"Fine, you can't come for Thanksgiving." Slade grinned.

Jagger's face fell. "But Mack makes the Hawaiian bread stuffing."

Slade kicked him the ball. "Exactly."

Matt was staring off in the distance, and then looked back at me. "Footwork drills, then a bit of two-on-two."

"Losers take ice baths!" Jagger announced.

I gave him the finger.

"Ah, I love your girl, just love her." Jagger chuckled to himself, and Matt and I both froze. Slade hid a laugh behind his hand while Jagger looked up and gave a lazy shrug. "What?"

"Nothing," I said quickly. "We doing this, or are you ladies just gonna talk all day?"

"Oh, we're doing this." Slade kicked the ball to me, I stopped it with my cleat. "Now get past me with your best, girl." He taunted me with a smirk, so I answered with a middle finger and swift fake to his left, then right, and then danced around him a bit before getting by and having to face Jagger.

I went at him hard and ate grass; one minute I was up, the next I was down. I jumped to my feet, wiped dirt on my shorts as sweat streamed down my chin. "Again."

I could feel Matt's smile from the sidelines as he blew his shiny new whistle at me.

We repeated drills for the next hour, and then we had to scrimmage, which wasn't going to be all that exciting since it was two of the league's best against Matt and me, not that we couldn't hold our own, but still.

"Ready for this, Cheetah Girl?" Matt kicked the ball to me as I stretched my hands in the air.

"Are you?" I teased.

He licked his lips, his gaze traveling from head to toe before giving me the smolder of all smolders.

All talk of Erik forgotten with one lazy look from Matt.

The guy wasn't human.

How did he do that to me?

I instantly felt the buzz from his look and then attacked. Fake and side kick ahead as Matt bounced it between both guys and then fired it back to me. It was like we could read each other's minds.

We had no plan, except to score.

And every single time I needed him to be downfield he was there, every time I needed a block he was there. It was incredible.

Like working with a teammate who knew me inside and out.

Now if only I could wipe the grin from my face as I careened toward Jagger.

He naturally blocked my kick and then gave me a *Nice try* look.

It didn't matter, because the journey to that kick had been invigorating. It had breathed life into my soul and made me think that maybe even with all this Erik business, things were going to be okay.

Chapter Twenty-Two

Matt

"It's like they knew we weren't going to win," I said as we stared at the two metal troughs filled to the brim with ice and water.

Slade wrapped a sweaty arm around me. "Should we light a candle for this special moment?"

"Chilled wine?" Jagger teased.

"Yes, please," Parker said sarcastically, chewing her bottom lip as she stared at the water. "It's going to feel good, it's going to feel good."

"Your girl's resorted to chanting," Slade joked.

He really needed to stop calling her that in front of me.

People might get the wrong idea.

Then again, she might get the right idea.

I jerked my shirt over my head and then pulled my joggers down to the ground. "Fuck it." I went all in to my chin and nearly lost my balls in the process.

Parker's movements were even faster as she got down to her sports bra and black Nike underwear and then jumped into the tub next to mine. Ice spilled over the edge.

Slade grinned down at both of us. "We should do this again next time."

And then he gave a serious look toward my bath, my knee. "Make sure you ice it later too, okay, man?"

"Yeah, yeah." I waved him off and closed my eyes as the door shut behind the maniacs.

"Must have been hard, getting an injury that severe," Parker said in a calm voice that got my full attention. It was cold as fuck in that tub. I couldn't even feel my spleen. At this point I wasn't even sure I had one.

Funny how she'd given me her entire life story from the past year, and all she knew about me was my job and that my sister was obsessed with shoes. "Yeah, knee injuries are never fun, especially public ones." She nodded her head as I gripped the side of the tub. "It's not really a sad story, just a normal tale of what happens when you turn one way and your body wants to turn the other way." I laughed. "I remember falling to the turf and thinking, 'Thank God,' which sounds horrible. I loved the game, I just knew that I wasn't cut out for it, not the way Slade and Jagger were. I loved the stats. I loved watching. And honestly, I made a few mistakes with some illegal substances. The team doctor slipped me some things that were supposed to help. Nobody found out but I hated myself for it. And then I realized I was playing a game I didn't enjoy anymore. I loved the behind-the-scenes stuff, so when I opened up my own agency it just seemed natural to represent my friends, and it grew from there."

"How many games did you play, you know, after the whole illegal-substances thing?" she asked in a backward way, skimming past *Why drugs, Matt?* It just made me want to talk more, open up, then pull her into my arms and ask her to stay.

"I played two seasons," I said thoughtfully. "I probably would have retired after three. My heart just wasn't in it, the drugs did the opposite of helping me since I felt so damn guilty. And Slade's talent—well, you've seen him play—is next level. That guy plays like you, he plays with his soul. I never did."

She was quiet except for water sloshing over the tub, and when I turned she was leaning over it. "You think I play with my soul?"

"I feel it." I locked eyes with her. "Every time you're out there, even during practice, you may yell at me, curse me—but you love every minute of suffering, admit it."

"I admit nothing." She smiled prettily. "Is our time almost up?"

"I hope it's soon, before I lose a toe or all function in my lower body."

"That would be a shame." I grinned and she added saucily, "Losing a toe."

I splashed her with cold water; it went directly into her face. "Whoops!"

"Whoops, my ass!" she yelled, splashing me harder, taking basically half of her water and tossing it in my direction. Before I had a chance to think about it, I was getting out of my tub and pulling her into the air and falling back into my tub with her in my arms. She squirmed, letting out a shriek before we splashed in together. I took her completely underwater.

She gasped for air and then smacked my frozen body with her hand.

"I feel nothing." I laughed harder.

Her teeth chattered as the sounds of footsteps neared, only to move past. I exhaled. Damn it, I was playing with fire, just begging to get burned over and over again.

The door opened. "Time's up!"

My first thought? Damn.

And I could tell it was hers too, as she slowly rose up over my body. I hooked my hands around her hips and moved to a sitting position as icy water slid down my body, down hers. I helped her out, setting her on her feet. She grasped my biceps for strength and then helped me out.

Both of us had chattering teeth.

Her lips were trembling and blue as she looked up at me with a question in her eyes. And like a coward, I backed away. "Let me get you a towel."

She hung her head. "Yeah, thanks."

I wrapped it around her body and held it there, steadying my breathing while she warmed up.

The sound of footsteps neared again.

I frowned. "Slade?"

No one answered.

She just shrugged. "Probably one of them or the janitor. It *is* getting late."

"Right." The hair on the back of my arms stood on end as I quickly grabbed my towel. "I'm going to hit the steam room."

"Ohhhh, me too!" She followed me before I could tell her that both of us in a small, enclosed space with sweat running down our bodies was a really bad idea.

Once we were both trapped inside the room, I sat down and almost whimpered when she sat down across from me. Next to me would have been better—next to me and I wouldn't have seen the sweat drip down her chin, I wouldn't be waiting for the fog to clear so I could count each successive drip onto her naked thigh.

I wouldn't be wondering what it would look like if she had nothing on at all.

I wouldn't feel like the worst sort of man for wanting to cover her body with mine, spread her legs, do all the dirty things my mind could conjure up—but it was Parker, hurt Parker. Parker who needed gentle. She needed that and time.

Disgusted with myself, I looked away.

"How did you manage to start the agency all on your own? I mean you only played a few seasons." Her voice filled the room like a soothing balm. I exhaled, inhaled, repeated the process, greedy for more air even if it smelled like her.

After a few seconds, I answered. "Willow and I both have trust funds. Our parents died when I was still in high school. I practically raised Willow, which is also why seeing her naked with Jagger made me want to grab a knife and throw it at him. I used the trust fund to put myself through college and open the agency. The rest is history, right along with Jagger's body once I find an accomplice."

Parker chuckled. "It's your job to be protective, that's what big brothers do. If you didn't try to physically harm her boyfriend I'd lose respect for you."

"Try telling her that."

"Trust me," she said in a low whisper. "She knows."

"And who protects you?" I wondered out loud before feeling like an ass for even saying it.

"Me. At least I try." Her voice was sad. "Not always successfully." She seemed to crawl into herself as she spoke. "My dad isn't really a huge supporter of my soccer career. We aren't close, at all. I think he forgets he even has a kid."

"Well, I have an opening, you know . . ." I joked and then backpedaled. "I mean not to be your dad, but to protect you, not like a brother . . ." Shit.

She didn't laugh.

"Parker?"

The fog cleared and then she was in front of me, hands on hips. "I'm not your sister, Matt."

"Fuck." I wiped my forehead. "Trust me, I know that."

"I don't want that sort of protection. Besides, if you're doing all the protecting, who's going to protect me from you?"

Called on my bullshit, I just stared her down. "You're right. I'm sorry."

"That"—she threw her hands in the air—"that wasn't an accusation! I just, I don't want you that way, I don't need a brother . . ."

Our eyes searched each other. "I don't think I can be anything else."

She backed away slowly.

"Parker . . ." I reached for her.

"No. It's fine. I get it . . ."

"You don't fucking get it," I said in a low voice and then stood. "I can't be anything to you, that's the truth. I respect you, I respect us. We have something here, I know it, you know it. I'm so damn proud of you and the strength that you have, how could I not want that? Don't you think I want more? Don't you think it tortures me at night? The way you taste? The feel of our palms pressed together, damn it, every touch from you, none of it is enough. You have to know that. But it doesn't matter, it doesn't matter that you drive me crazy in every way possible."

"Matt—"

"I won't be him."

"You aren't him."

"You're wrong," I said sadly. "I would be just like him if I took what I wanted just because I wanted it."

"You wouldn't be taking," she whispered.

I hung my head. "I'd be crossing a professional line that I've flirted with for over a week, Parker. Don't tempt me, it's not fair."

"*That* sounded like him," she said sadly.

She got up, grabbed her bag, and then walked to the door. Her footsteps haunted me, they sounded like a clock ticking, reminding me that whatever this was, was over. The door opened and clicked shut.

And I knew I was alone.

And I'd messed up.

Again.

Chapter Twenty-Three

When I took a shower that night, my self-worth circled the drain right along with all the dirt and sweat from my body. And when I went to practice the next day, I felt sluggish, my body weighed down by guilt.

"Parker!" Matt yelled. "Focus!"

It was our last practice. I couldn't focus on anything but the fact that he'd said he was just like Erik, and then it was like he accused me of . . . seducing him.

Like I couldn't help but make every man want me.

When I just wanted him.

When for the first time in my life I wanted more than a goal, more than to make it on a professional team, I just wanted him to want me back in a way that was real, purely us. And I knew that I was asking a lot, so I gave him chances, what girl wouldn't? I knew I had baggage, so I was giving him a free pass, and the accusations against me weren't exactly helping. I just wanted him to look past it all and see me. I needed him to see me.

I squeezed my eyes shut against the onslaught of tears.

"Stop." Matt blew the whistle. "We're done for the day."

My head jerked up as panic seized my chest. Was he giving up on me? Was he firing me as his client? "No, no, no, I'll try harder!"

"No." His voice was stern but his expression was soft. "I've worked you too hard. It's fine . . . you need a break, you need . . . fun."

Why the heck did he look guilty?

I crossed my arms. "Fun? As in, I need to go to a theme park? Shopping? What do you mean fun?"

He let out an exhausted sigh. "Just put the attitude on hold, and maybe pause the sarcasm. We planned something for you, a sort of party to say good job for all the hellish training and dealing with an asshole as your agent, coach, and friend."

I smiled. "Really?"

"Yeah, really." Why did he still look guilty?

"We invited some of Jagger and Slade's teammates, a few of them said they knew you from college. I thought it would be fun for you to hang out with people . . ." He swallowed and added with a rasp, "Your age."

I jerked back. "Oh."

His smile seemed forced, dark circles lined his eyes like he hadn't slept in days. Why hadn't I noticed that before? "I had Mack plan the whole thing. We rented out one of the rooms at the country club, got a DJ. Things are about to get lit."

"Don't say *lit*, you can't get away with it like Jagger can," I teased, even though I felt like crying.

He nodded, then grabbed my hand and squeezed it. "I'm proud of you."

He dropped that same hand.

I clenched it to make sure I wasn't wrong.

And then Matt Kingston turned around and walked back toward the gear and gathered it up, leaving me standing in the middle of a field with a broken heart.

Other guys.

Guys my age.

He was proud.

He was done.

And I was devastated.

◆　◆　◆

I was in another pretty dress.

A drink was pressed into my hand.

It tasted bland.

Willow had done my hair, which fell in loose curls around my shoulders. I was wearing a backless dress with a pair of her Jimmy Choos that made my legs look even longer than they already were. I didn't feel like a princess, though. More like a lamb out for the slaughter.

Guys from college recognized me, alright.

They recognized me as the girl that punched her coach and was rumored to have seduced him in the locker room in order to try to make it to pro. Cheers.

A few of them were nice to me.

One of them paid me too much attention. I couldn't remember his name, mainly because I didn't like the way he kept staring at my chest.

"I need another drink," I told Willow as I walked over to the punch and bypassed it for the bar. "Vodka, double, on the rocks, with a lime," I said in an anxiety-filled voice.

"Are you drinking on a school night?" an amused voice said from behind me.

I turned around and gave Jagger a middle-finger salute. "And to think they let you out of the retirement home! How's it feel to be free?"

He just laughed. "Hey, as long as my dick still works."

I made a face. "Maybe don't say that around Matt."

"Your cheeks are puffy again," he said, suddenly serious.

I shifted on my feet. "Thought makeup hid that."

"Nothing hides sadness the way we want it to, does it?"

"Why are you suddenly finding your tiny heart and using it to have a conversation with me?" I wondered out loud.

"I like Willow. She's fun. She's carefree. She's young, spontaneous, hysterical. But, people like you, people like us," he said in a mysterious tone, "we're forced to age a lot faster than we'd like . . . I'd say you may even be older than our friend Matt."

I snorted.

"He likes you." Jagger shrugged. "More than he likes me and Slade combined, and he gets millions from us. He would fucking give me both his kidneys and never look back."

"Well, that was probably before you started dating his sister."

"Ouch." Jagger winced and then wrapped an arm around me. "You can't kill a guy for trying to do the right thing, and Matt, he's trying to do the right thing here. You're his client. I'm not a dumbass, I see the way he looks at you, the way you look at him. He's trying to do good by you, Parker."

I looked down at my heels and shrugged, hating that Matt was being the bigger person, the good guy. How ironic. I'd always wanted a guy like Matt, but now, now my past and his morals kept us apart.

"I don't know what happened, Parker. He still refuses to tell me why he looks at you like he's starving but refuses to take a bite, even though we all know it's not going to kill his career or yours. Would a relationship between you two be frowned upon? Yes. Is it illegal? Hell no. But something happened, I'm assuming with you, and he didn't break that trust. He never would. He's good, the best. He's just . . . good, which I can't say for everyone I've known in this league . . ."

My heart began a staccato beat, and I looked up with wide eyes as he ran a hand over his buzzed hair.

"I knew your old coach, Erik, and caught him with an underage girl once. We played together early on, back before Slade and I had our huge falling-out. Point is, he's not a good guy, so if you punched him, you had a damn good reason. And it makes me wonder if that's why Matt's turned so noble. When you're interested you don't just stop playing the game."

"But he got hurt . . ." I offered lamely.

"Hah!" He grinned. "I like you. No, I mean players. Ladies' men. A guy like Matt doesn't just put everything on hold for anyone. He doesn't make it personal, but he made it personal with you for a reason. Maybe it's time you reminded him why." He took a sip of his drink. "And if he asks, Willow and I aren't getting busy in the wine cellar."

"Ew!" I shoved him away. "No details!"

"She wore really high heels for a reason, Cheetah Girl."

I glared.

"Go show him your moves." He chuckled. "But finish your liquid courage first, because Matt's a hard one to crack, and believe me, brother must be hard as fuck these days."

I scrunched up my nose.

He just shrugged and sauntered off.

And that's when Slade made his way over.

"Oh good, another pep talk. Anything you want to add to the train wreck that Jagger left in his wake?"

"Who?" Slade's eyes were so pretty it was almost hard to focus. "I was just going to say you should probably put Matt out of his misery and mine. He's been texting me every night, and Mack said she was going to change my phone number if he didn't stop."

"Texting you to what? Hang out?"

"No, have a pillow fight," he said drily. "He was drunk last night."

"So?" I downed the rest of my drink.

"He's always in control, doesn't get drunk just to get drunk. He always has a reason for everything, and he told me what it was . . ."

I leaned forward.

"Hey, I don't gossip." Slade held up his hands. "But I'm pretty sure if you get him to dance with you, you'll find out."

"So dancing's going to solve this?"

"No." Slade's gaze turned serious. "An equal amount of communication, sex, and hydration will, though."

I exhaled.

"And off you go . . ." Slade gave me a light tap on the back as I made my way over to where Matt was stewing.

Music pumped through the dark room. There was a huge dance floor in the middle under two chandeliers. Nearly two hundred people including old teammates, possible new ones, coaches, and other agents were in attendance. Basically, Matt had set up the party to be a relaunch of my career, and already I'd chatted with other coaches who were begging me to come to a tryout after Seattle.

And every single time I had to fake my excitement.

Because I'd fallen in love with Washington.

And everything it entailed.

Matt was standing near the wall talking with one of the Reign coaches.

"And there she is." His face was tired but he was still beautiful— angry and beautiful like when we first met.

I smiled at that, which seemed to only make him scowl more.

"We were just talking about you." Paul Willard was respected throughout the league, and I had always liked him. "Are you ready for Sunday?"

I took a deep breath. "As ready as I'll ever be. I just wanted to thank you for taking a chance on me, I know you didn't have to."

Matt stiffened next to me while Paul's smile softened. "We would have been missing out, and that's the truth."

I nodded. "I'll do my best."

"I know you will," he agreed. "Alright, I should go find the wife, she said something about a slow dance."

Matt laughed. "Good luck."

Paul chuckled and left us alone, in that dark corner near the dance floor.

Rachel Van Dyken

"You look nice." I gulped.

His eyebrows rose in dark humor. "I look like shit, but thanks."

"Do you feel like shit too?"

He bit down on his lip and then looked away. "Aren't you having fun?"

"A blast, I totally got hit on by the cutest guy." Matt's head whipped in my direction so fast it almost came off his body. "Gotcha."

He clenched his jaw, I could see the vein. And for some reason it made me happy. I smiled and held out my hand. "Want to dance?"

"Not really, no." He stared me down with a scowl.

"Please? As friends?"

I knew I was winning when he sighed again, set down his drink, and then led me onto the dark dance floor as Liam Payne's song came on. "Familiar" was a mix of hip hop and salsa, I loved it. Matt looked ready to crawl away screaming. I wondered if he was ready to call it a night or just uncomfortable. Sometimes I couldn't get a read on him, and it killed me to wonder if the distance was because he truly didn't want me or because he was afraid of the consequences of wanting me.

I tugged him close just as Willow, Jagger, Slade, and Mack joined us on the floor dancing.

The rest of the Sounders must have been drunk enough to think dancing was a good idea because soon the dance floor was so crowded we were almost pushed toward the wall, surrounded by dancing bodies and blanketed in darkness.

I grabbed Matt's hands, put them on my hips, and swiveled with the music; he closed his eyes and moved with me. The surprising part was that he could move. Then again most athletes I knew were good dancers, but he was great.

I circled him and then turned and thrust my ass against him as I lifted my hands above my head. All I could hear was cursing from his mouth. I considered it a win as he ran his hands down my arms and across my stomach, pulling me against him as I bent over and shimmied with the rhythm, rocking into his hips. Feeling him press against me almost made me trip. The guy was packing.

I turned around, his face was stone-cold sober like he refused to give anything away as we danced together. He put distance between us, and then I took that distance right back.

We danced like we argued.

And I refused to lose.

When I looked over my shoulder it was to see Slade jerk his head toward me. What? He wanted me to seduce my agent on the dance floor? In front of everyone?

I had a better idea.

Wine cellar.

Jagger wasn't there.

Did that mean it was empty?

A tortured look crossed Matt's face when I wrapped my arms around his neck, and yet he kept a respectable space between us. I smirked, which just made him scowl even more.

I'd never taken control of anything with Erik.

He never gave me that option.

He just took.

Spread his poison.

And took some more.

At least with Matt, I was going to go down swinging.

I fell against him and winced.

"What's wrong?" He gripped my body with both hands, while I lied into his ear.

"I think it's my ankle."

"Fuck!" He wrapped an arm around me. "Can you walk?"

"Yeah, just need to go somewhere, not here." I was a horrible liar, but he must have believed the pain on my face as we slowly walked out of the private banquet hall.

I immediately saw a sign for the wine cellar and turned to my right. I was walking just fine.

In fact, I was almost sprinting.

He chased after me.

When we stopped in front of the wine cellar, I nearly choked. There were private little rooms everywhere, maybe tasting rooms? But each one had a crazy-looking fur blanket, couches, tables, and candles lit everywhere. No wonder Jagger wanted to end up in here; it was like your own private castle.

I tugged Matt into the first room and closed the doors, then locked them.

He paced like a caged animal in front of me. "Parker."

His voice was raspy, filled with exactly zero self-control.

"Yes?"

"Is your ankle really hurt?"

"No. But my heart is . . . you should probably start making it better." I put my hands on my hips.

He gaped. "Listen—"

"I'd rather not."

I slammed my mouth against his.

And prayed he'd respond.

Chapter Twenty-Four

Matt

I had zero restraint left.

I'd used it all trying not to peel her clothes off her body when we were dancing. I hauled her into my arms and drank, sucking on her tongue first, then deepening the kiss as I pulled the halter part of her dress free. More like tore it. I wasn't in control anymore as I nipped her lips with my teeth and tugged the rest of the dress down to her hips.

"Does this mean you forgive me about the ankle?" Parker laughed as she worked the buttons down my shirt and then spread her palms over my naked chest as she shoved it off my body.

I gripped her by the wrists. "Not even a little bit. You scared the hell out of me. Next time just . . ." Our chests heaved as my eyes fell to the sexy-as-fuck black strapless bodice. It was connected just above her ass in the back and thrust her breasts in my face. "Just . . ." I licked my lips as visions of exploring the valley between her tits had my entire body pulsing with excitement. I would do that, I would do so many things before this night was over.

"Just?" She put her hands on her hips and stepped back. "What? You like this?"

I cupped her ass and tugged her toward me. Holding her against me felt better than I could ever have possibly imagined. My length throbbed against her dress, too many clothes stood between us, but I had to get a better look at that bodice.

"It's . . ." I lifted a fingertip and ran it down the curve of her breast and up the other. "Teasing me."

"The bodice?"

"Yeah, I can't decide if I want to rip it apart and buy you a new one or slowly undo each hook and torture myself with what I'll find underneath."

She sucked in a breath and then turned away from me. "I choose torture."

I chuckled darkly against her neck. "Why am I not surprised?" The scent of candles and luscious wine filled the air, and the scent of her skin, the taste of whiskey on my tongue mixed with each kiss I stole from her back. Each hook I undid had me ready to explode.

A small part of me still felt like I was taking advantage, but then she'd sigh my name, her head falling forward as I trailed kisses down her back.

She was mine.

Fuck whoever saw.

My body tensed and throbbed at the final hook. After tossing her bodice to the side and slowly pulling her dress over her hips, I stared at her ass long enough for Parker to look over her shoulder. "You gonna make it, old man?"

"Call me old and I really will spank you," I growled, running a palm down her lower back and resting it against one perfect cheek. I pinched.

She let out a squeal and turned in my arms, facing me the way I'd imagined since I first saw her on my doorstep with freshly baked cookies.

"Tell me this isn't wrong." I swallowed against the dryness in my throat, the intense need to taste her, to claim her, to calm this erratic beating in my chest, this roaring in my blood that said she'd always been mine, that this was the most right thing I'd ever do.

Her lush mouth pressed together in a secret smile, and then she was walking backward to the couch, her naked skin kissed the fur blanket as she pulled me on top of her.

Our mouths met with a pent-up frenzy I'd never experienced before. With a cheeky smile against my lips, she reached for my trousers.

I batted her hand away. "Not yet."

"Yes yet." She laughed.

"Who has the whistle, Parker?"

"Who has the boobs, Matt?"

"Touché." I laughed and then dipped my head to pay homage to the most gorgeous pair of tits I'd ever seen. I sucked on one nipple, testing her out, wanting to see her lips part with each swirl of my tongue, each pleasure-filled bite.

"Ah." She bit down on her lip and shook her head. "I like that, a lot."

My body tightened as my balls drew up, sweat collected on my upper lip as our mouths joined again, not because I was overexerting myself but because the candles mixed with what was left of my self-control were wreaking havoc on my body temperature.

I lowered my fingers to her bare core, and before I even had a chance to do anything, she was moving against my palm.

I clenched my teeth.

"Matt."

"Yeah."

"Foreplay's boring."

"What?"

"Not you. Just foreplay." She moved against my hand again and then grabbed my arm and thrust against my palm. "I want you. I've only ever just wanted you. Not your fingers. Not your mouth. I want you. Inside me. Deep. Now. I want to be yours."

I'd heard of guys losing control.

I'd never experienced that blinding animalistic explosion. It consumed my body as I stood, bringing her with me. Her hands jerked down my pants and briefs, shoes were kicked off, and then I was backing her against one of the chairs, lifting her onto the table, and entering her in one smooth thrust.

"Matt!" She clung to me as her body tightened, her head tossed back like she almost couldn't take me.

"Right here, baby, stay right here." She tasted like vodka and longing, wet and scorching all at the same time as I thrust into her again, holding her there, pinning her against the table. I made my way onto the table, my body plastered against hers, all skin and sweat, as our eyes connected.

"Deeper." She arched beneath me.

I moved inside her and wondered if there had ever been anything so perfect as that moment. She squeezed her eyes shut and opened them as we moved in sync and I raked a kiss down her neck. We fucked like we played. In perfect harmony. I should have known it would be like that.

Like she could read my mind.

Like I could read hers.

"I knew it would be like this. It should be like this." She clung to me, clamored for me as she wrapped an arm around my neck then one leg around my waist.

I rose over her one last time as I felt her walls suck me dry, and when I saw her crazed eyes roll back, I pressed a finger between our bodies, hitting her sweet spot just in time to watch her climax.

"What was that?" she asked in wonder, panting after her release.

But I wasn't done yet, not by a long shot. I eased out of her then pulled her down the edge of the table and carried her over to the couch, laying her on her back with the pillow beneath her legs. "Aren't we—"

I sank deep, she was so slick that I was surprised I could still focus as I hiked up her legs with my arms, giving me a better angle, a deeper angle. Her eyes widened. "Holy shit, what is—"

I silenced her with a kiss, loving her innocent expression, hating that a monster once took it from her.

"Foreplay," I said against her mouth. "Trust me, you want foreplay. You want to be ready for me, for this, for us." I moved my hips in a circular motion then gripped her ass, driving deeper as she bent up and grabbed my face, pressing a kiss to it just as I felt her body pulse around mine. I thrust one last time, my control once again at its end.

She collapsed against the fur blanket, a smile on her face.

"What?" Why was I winded? What the hell?

"I guess you're not old," was her answer as I grabbed a nearby pillow that we were most definitely going to burn, and tossed it in her direction, still inside her, still feeling the afterpulses of our bodies.

No regrets.

None.

And when she said, "I want to sleep in your bed."

I couldn't get her dressed fast enough.

Because I suddenly saw it as ours.

Chapter Twenty-Five

I didn't want to stay for the rest of the party. I wanted to go home with Matt. I was almost embarrassed that when I thought of home, it was his home that came to mind, and him.

Both of them a package deal.

I smiled to myself as I retied my halter top and smoothed down my dress, careful to make sure there wasn't any evidence of what we'd just done.

I turned in time for Matt to hand me a glass of wine and lean in, like it was normal to lean in and kiss me.

Did sex make that normal now?

Could we do that?

Was it allowed?

Giddy, I kissed him back as he moaned into my mouth. God, his wine-infused tongue felt like velvet against mine. Our mouths danced along each other, and then I clung to his chest with my free hand, just as someone cleared their throat.

Had there even been footsteps?

Jagger stood there, stupid grin on his face.

"What are you?" Matt glared. "A fucking ninja?"

He grinned wide. "Willow will be here in less than thirty seconds. What to do, what to do . . . I mean on one hand . . ."

I grumbled as he held out one hand.

"I could just yell like Matt did when I was caught with my pants down, literally. I could tell her that her best friend was hooking up with her brother . . . hmmm." He held out his other hand. "And in this hand . . ." He lifted his hand to his lips, mimed zipping them, whistled, tossed the imaginary key into the air, then swallowed it.

"You done?" Matt asked in a bored tone.

Jagger crossed his arms. "I want to date your sister."

"Absolutely not." Matt's teeth clenched, every muscle in his body strained beneath his shirt. I was surprised he was able to hold his wineglass without breaking it over Jagger's head. "She's off-limits."

"Well, shit." Jagger smiled wide. "I guess I'll just let her know that her best friend, your houseguest, and, well, I wasn't going to say it but I think I will now, her friend's mentor, were just in here ripping each other's clothes off, screaming profanities, and getting busy on the table." He jerked his head to the wood. "I think your bodies missed a spot, you were trying to get every inch, right?"

Matt shared a look with me. "We'll tell her."

My anxiety spiked.

"Just not today." He sighed. "One date, you can go out on one date, and if you suddenly elope or she ends up pregnant, I'm going to throw you off my balcony and claim it was a war crime. Your grandma should be helpful with that."

Jagger burst out laughing just as loud footsteps made their way down the corridor. "Hey, baby, you ready to—Matt!" Willow stopped short.

"Nice red wine, isn't it?" Jagger crossed his arms. "So . . . robust."

I almost choked on my next sip then set the wine down on the table. "You know what? I'm exhausted."

"How sudden." Jagger winked.

I sent him a *Stop it* look while Matt grinned like he was suddenly thrilled at the prospect of Jagger and his sister alone. "Actually, Willow, Jagger was just telling us about his love for shoes. You should tell him about your trip to Paris, I'm sure he'd love every detail. In fact, you guys stay as long as you want."

"Oh, we will." Jagger pulled Willow close.

Matt sighed and elbowed Jagger as we both walked by.

Willow made a beeline for the wine.

Jagger grabbed my wrist. "Careful."

"Weren't you just encouraging this?" I hissed.

"Doesn't mean you shouldn't still tread carefully." He winked. "Have fun tonight."

"Already did."

"Night's not over," he said, making my heart thump like a party in my chest.

I clung to Matt's side as we made our way back down the hall.

And then reality set in.

Because when he opened the door, his hand fell from mine.

His posture stiffened.

Right.

Athlete.

Coach.

Professional.

I forced a smile on my face as we said our good-byes to people around the room. I was exhausted by the time I grabbed my coat. The car was brought around. Matt opened my door, and I got in and waited for something, anything to remind me of the magic from the wine cellar.

But he didn't even reach for my hand.

I felt the sting of tears.

Had it just been physical?

It was so much more to me.

More than I'd ever admit out loud.

Because those words held power, and I'd learned my lesson—never give another person all of yours.

There was something thrilling and terrifying about pulling up to a dark house with a man who just had his mouth all over your body.

Did you just walk into the kitchen and ask if he was up for a midnight snack then drop your clothes?

Or was it more normal than that? Did you walk in, watch TV in your pajamas, and then end up on top of one another?

Or did we just go to bed.

Him with a book.

Me with my ear buds and a magazine?

By the time the car rolled to a stop, the garage door slowly going down, I was almost sick to my stomach. I had dated in college.

But not men like this.

Not powerful men who had their own houses, businesses. Men who could have their pick of any woman in the world.

I hadn't been thinking all those things when I danced with him, when I took Matt to the wine cellar. All I'd thought about was him. I needed him. Only him.

I exhaled and opened my car door, nearly banging Matt in the face. "Nice, sex and suddenly you get violent?" Matt laughed. "Is this normal behavior for you?"

I grinned up at him as he helped me out of the car. "Describe normal?"

He dropped my hand. I tried not to look as disappointed as I felt. "Good point."

I ducked my head shyly and walked into the house, the loud clicking from my heels wasn't helping the nervousness wracking my body.

And suddenly Matt was behind me.

I closed my eyes as his hands traveled down my arms, and then he was drawing me back against his body. It was just us and the darkness in that living room. I would be okay. I had him. He had me.

"What were you thinking?" he whispered as he trailed hot, lingering kisses down the side of my neck.

"Hmm? What?"

He gripped my hips tight and turned me around to face him, his eyes drilled into me with fury. "What the hell were you thinking?"

I gasped. "I wasn't really thinking, thinking wasn't really part of the scenario when I was naked beneath you."

"Anyone could have found us. Your reputation—" He held me tight, his eyes locked onto mine with an intensity that took my breath away. "I don't give a fuck about me, I care about you. Next time you decide to push me past my self-control, we need to be alone, unless you want the world to believe the worst about you, and Parker, I don't think I would survive that. I know I wouldn't. I could live with a lot of things, but people not seeing who you truly are because they're so busy judging actions they don't understand—I will not, would not, handle that well. I would rip apart every newspaper, every magazine article. I'd torch the world until they saw your truth, your beauty, your heart."

Tears filled my eyes. "And I wouldn't let you."

"I would try."

"I'd leave before you ruined yourself over me," I whispered sadly. "But the fact that you'd be willing to do it makes me want to cry, and nobody should cry after sex. It's weird."

"So weird," he agreed while I quickly swiped my cheeks and smiled. "But understandable."

"Maybe." I swallowed the lump in my throat. "I don't like being emotional."

"Nooooo," he teased. "Really? I had no idea."

I smacked him on the shoulder.

"Violence is more your answer. I'm surprised you didn't tie me to that Buddha sculpture with a piece of rope licorice, ride me, and call me bitch."

I burst out laughing. "You are such an asshole!"

He kissed me.

Once, twice.

I lost count of the heated kisses in his living room, in his house, in his home.

I jumped, wrapped my arms around his neck, and deepened the kiss while he slid his hands up my thighs, gripping my bare ass as he slowly walked us past the guest room.

To his bed.

"As promised," he whispered against the crook of my neck. "Now what?"

"Now," I exhaled, taking in his bedroom. He had a fireplace in the corner by the master bathroom you could tell he was still remodeling. A flat-screen hung on the wall, and pictures and decorations added to an aesthetically beautiful masculine bedroom that made me think about Pier 1 and campfires. "Now we test out this . . ." I reached for his bed, just to touch the chocolate duvet, but his hands were on me already, lifting me into the air and dropping me back on the mattress as he started unbuttoning his shirt.

I watched him, licking my lips as he shrugged out of the shirt. The man's body was . . . well, I wanted to lick every single rivet of muscle, I wanted to run my mouth down his six-pack and then see how many licks it would take to travel to my final destination.

His smug grin told me he knew, oh he knew how sexy he was, how overwhelming it was when all I saw was muscular, tight skin I wanted to rake my fingernails over to leave a mark and claim him as mine.

"Not old . . ." I found myself saying, my voice coming out hoarsely. "Just a very built man."

"Not old," he agreed, reaching for the button of his trousers. "Needy, though, I'm very needy. I don't think you realize how many times I've stopped outside your door, and yet when I say it out loud . . ."

"Sounds creepy, a bit. Yeah." I laughed and then grasped his pants and tugged him closer. I could see every hard inch of him straining toward me, teasing me. "I would have let you in."

"What?" His eyes were lazily focused on me as I slowly ran my hands down his hips, touching the skin there, running my fingers in slow circles while he let out a moan.

"I would have let you in," I said honestly. "Though you would have had to leave the whistle at the door."

He choked out a laugh and then groaned. "Your hands, they feel so good . . ."

"I wanted this," I confessed without looking at him. "I wanted us."

"Now that you have this . . . us"—he cupped my face—"what are you going to do?"

I grinned up at him. "I'm a taker."

"I like that."

"And right now . . ." Other than getting taken advantage of by my coach and then sleeping with a boyfriend in college, I was lacking in sexual experience. But it didn't matter. It was shocking to my very core that I could look at Matt and feel like I was everything to him, like this meant something. The look on his face expressed everything his words hadn't yet said. He cared, he wanted, he wanted me just as bad as I did him. I was so damn afraid and he made me brave. He made me want to spend endless hours naked, longing, licking. And it was all because he cared, he gave me hope, he was a partner. An equal. . . . "Right now, I want to taste you like you tasted me."

"Whatever you want," he grated. "I'll give it to you."

"Whatever I want?" I teased.

"Everything." His face sobered. "Everything."

"Nobody's ever offered me everything."

"I am. And I keep my promises—besides, someone said they wanted to sleep in my bed."

"Well, I mean you have to be in it too . . ." I slid his trousers down over his hips, eye level with something so smooth and beautiful that I let out a girly sigh, one so unlike me that I was almost embarrassed. I eyed him as I lowered my mouth.

He gripped my wrists with his hands. "Yeah." He swayed on his feet. "I'll be in it. We just have to figure out Willow."

"Let's not talk about your sister in between tastes." I swirled my tongue around him and then winked. "Like wine tasting, only better."

"Except the cork is already threatening to go off." He shook his head. "Later. I've been tortured by every fucking look you sent my way, every argument, every outfit, every practice, every morning since you first arrived at my door with cookies."

"Ah, he's an asshole when he's happy too?"

"Apparently he's an asshole no matter what." He flipped me onto my back and kicked off his pants. "And now, now I get to make up for it by taking my time."

"Oh." A warm blush spread over my face. "That's okay, you don't have to—"

My dress was suddenly over my head, my backless bodice was on, but I was naked from the waist down and his mouth was feasting on me like a girl always imagines, with the same precision a striker eyes downfield, the same artful movement from left to right, a fake, kick deep.

"Aaaagghrmmmphhh!" I screamed into a pillow. "Matt!"

"Sorry, couldn't decipher that, also I'm super busy right now . . ." He chuckled against my sensitive skin. "Hmmmm, wanted to taste you so bad, knew it would be like this . . . fucking knew it . . ."

I squeezed my thighs as he took me higher. I felt my body shamelessly move against him.

"That's it, baby," he encouraged, and then I wasn't hearing anything but the sound of my own heart as I felt my release and nearly came off the mattress and disappeared into thin air.

"Get there."

"I can't—"

"You scored the winning goal at the championships two years ago, you were wearing your hair in a braid, and all I kept thinking when I looked at your tape was, 'Damn, that woman is too beautiful for words,' and now I know—now I know, you're beautiful everywhere, inside, outside." He licked, he sucked. "You're perfect."

I grabbed his head with one hand and let out a scream.

"All you needed . . ." He looked up at me, slowly crawled up my body like a panther ready to stake claim on its prey. "Was someone who cared."

"No." I cupped his face. "I just needed you."

His eyes darted to my mouth.

I lunged for him, tasting myself on him, tasting us, and I forgot all about my past.

It was just us.

In his bedroom.

In his house.

I'd begged Matt for a future without even realizing it would never be complete without him in it.

I didn't say I love you.

Not with my words.

But with every kiss, with every touch, I tried to tell him what was in my heart.

I pushed him onto his back and straddled him.

His eyes widened a fraction of an inch as I moved over him, taking him in, sinking down slowly as our eyes locked, breathing quickened.

So many tiny breaths.

So many small moans.

Growls.

Touches.

A million of them between us, all meaning the same thing, more and more.

He gripped me with one hand as I held his other above his head, riding him, loving him, feeling our thighs slide together in sync as sweat heated our bodies.

His teeth clenched. "Can't hold back."

"Never asked you to." I lowered my head. The motion created a secret curtain between our mouths as they met gently, as we moved together.

It was just us in that moment.

Nobody else.

And then his eyes were wild as he moved with me. I took him deep as a pulsing sensation shot through us.

There.

Perfect.

Us.

"Matt?" My voice was hoarse, had I been yelling that much?

His hands were still on my ass. "Yeah?"

"I really, really like your bed."

He slapped me on one ass cheek and let out an exhausted laugh. "Just don't kick me out of it anytime soon, alright?"

"Just don't bring your whistle into the bedroom, and I won't have a reason to."

"Valid point. I'm burning all whistles. Does that mean every time I don't have a whistle we have sex? Because I could really get on board with that."

I smacked his naked chest while he burst out laughing and pulled me to my side, kissing my neck from behind.

"You're beautiful."

Being called beautiful by Matt was the highest high, because Matt didn't give out compliments, so when he said it, I believed it.

"I like your six-pack?" was my counter offer.

Which just got me more tickling of my side.

And then I sobered as he held me close. "Is it wrong to ask what happens next?"

"Life, Parker. Life happens next."

"Yeah?"

He kissed my temple. "Yeah, but first sleep."

I yawned. "And you'll be here . . . in your bed."

"I'm here."

"Home," came out of my mouth before I could stop the words.

"Home, Parker. Home."

Chapter Twenty-Six

MATT

I couldn't remember the last time I woke up with such a huge grin on my face. I turned on my side to see Parker still sleeping. Damn, she was beautiful. Her hair was a mess all over the pillow like she was trying to claim ownership with each strand.

And it made me that much more determined to keep her there.

She fit.

We fit.

I wasn't sure how.

Or why.

And I didn't know what the hell I was going to tell the press if they ever caught wind of our relationship, which just meant we needed to deal with this Erik business once and for all. He was threatening, stalking, and bordering on being a complete sociopath. And the last thing we needed was for her to feel powerless or afraid again. I was more concerned about her mental state than I was about her position on any team. In my mind I could do anything, create a miracle, get her to play anywhere; the issue was him, it had always been him. He was the root problem, and I needed to destroy him as soon as possible.

Starting with a phone call this morning to let the LA team know she wasn't interested, especially after last night.

The Seattle Reign were almost all in. All she had to do was be her charming self, a.k.a. kick ass, have a killer tryout, and it would be a done deal.

I was giving her a rest day so she would be fresh for tryouts, but knowing Parker, she'd want to at least go for a run.

And it would be normal for her coach to go with her, right?

I quickly dressed and put on my running shoes then jogged into the kitchen to make breakfast.

"So . . ." Willow's voice had me nearly tripping over my own feet. She was sitting at the breakfast bar with a newspaper in front of her face so I couldn't read her expression. "I hope I'm not intruding."

"Intruding?" Shit. "Nope. Not at all. Just headed out for a run in a few."

She slammed the newspaper down. She was fresh faced and wearing a Seattle Sounders sweatshirt.

I pointed. "Is that Jagger's?"

"I am NOT making that whore breakfast!" she screeched, turning her head to me.

I opened my mouth to respond then jerked back. "Fuck, is that a hickey?" I roared.

"I heard that slut's screams twice last night! Twice! I almost had to get ear plugs." She threw her hands in the air.

Wait a second. Whose pants were those?

"Those aren't yours." I grabbed a coffee mug and stared down her obviously too-big black Nike sweat pants.

"I can't believe you!" She paced, completely ignoring me. "You just bring home the first skank you can find! Poor Parker had to listen to that all night long, and you know she likes you! What the hell is wrong with you, Matt!" She turned and reached for a magazine and rolled it up, which revealed another hickey on the other side of her neck.

"How long did that sick bastard suck on your neck! We aren't vampires!" I hollered. "Where is he!" I tried getting past her. "Jagger! You sick motherfucker! I said one date! Not a feast!"

Parker chose that moment to make an appearance in nothing but one of my T-shirts. Jagger came out of the shared bathroom. They took one look at each other.

And fucking high-fived.

I groaned into my hands while Willow jumped into the air. "YOU WERE THE SKANK LAST NIGHT?"

"I wasn't that loud!" Parker said defensively. "And it's not like—"

"I get to be your maid of honor!" Willow announced, performing a little twirl.

"Aw, you guys are getting married?" Jagger winked and then sidestepped me. "Need some coffee, bro. Your sister's an animal."

A headache throbbed at the base of my skull. "Wait, Willow, why are *you* happy, you just found out I was with . . ." I felt my face pale and then felt guilt start to pulse through my body. "Will . . ."

"No." She held up her hand. "And yes, I'm happy. Happy with Jagger." I held my groan in. "And I'm happy for you." She frowned. "Wait, aren't you happy? I've only been trying to get you guys together since we accidentally"—she made air quotes—"moved in under weird circumstances."

Jagger chomped down on an apple next to me. "She's a manipulative, evil mastermind. Seen her shoe collection? Huge, it's huge, not normal." Another large bite. "I think they hold her secrets."

I took a long, soothing breath and locked eyes with Parker, who burst out laughing so hard tears started streaming down her cheeks.

"Willow, what the hell?"

She grinned over at me. "I know you, I know what you need, and I've known for years that the one girl you need in your life just needed to be groomed by me. You know, a few short skirts, some makeup—"

Parker snorted.

"Or," Willow said, grinning, "just bringing her around so you could see what I see, what everyone sees: the most amazing woman you've ever met."

"Likewise," Jagger grumbled, pulling Willow in for a kiss.

I stared.

At everyone.

Mouth ajar.

And then . . .

"Coffee?" Parker laughed, walking by me, grabbing my shirt with her fist, and dragging me along. I loved it. How the hell was my sister so smart? Huh, maybe she should be an agent. I shook my head in disbelief.

"Dessert," I finally grumbled against her mouth, suddenly unable to keep my hands off her. I mean she was wearing my shirt, *my* shirt.

"Stop that!" Willow yelled. "Just because I wanted it to happen doesn't mean I wanted to see it live and in person."

We broke apart, smiling.

"Oh, and by the way, Jagger and I are dating." She blew a kiss to Jagger.

"Surprise, asshole." He finger-waved at me then flipped me off. I almost charged him and broke every finger off his hand, but her smile stopped me, Willow's smile. The way she looked at him was the same way I looked at Parker, and I couldn't fault my sister for wanting that, because I think deep down we'd both always wanted that, the feeling of coming home, of partnership. I took a sip of coffee and purposely ignored his taunt.

"What? No yelling anymore?" Jagger almost sounded disappointed.

"Nope." I grinned wide, suddenly thrilled that someone else could corral her. "Because now you get to deal with the shoe problem. Good thing you're worth a shit ton of money, you're gonna need it."

"He exaggerates." Willow rolled her eyes.

"Shoes." Jagger snorted. "How much can one pair of shoes cost?"

"Her last pair cost more than my first car in high school," Parker said helpfully, causing Jagger to choke.

"Baby, I came from Russia. Grandma taught me to save, you know she survived the Cold War and all," Jagger said.

Cold War? Parker mouthed while I hit him in the back of the head.

"Hurt her, and I hurt you," I threatened.

"Then who takes care of Parker if she gets hurt?" Jagger fired back then held out his fist for her to bump. "Tell you what, I'm adopting you, and now if he tries to break your heart, I'll break his leg, cool?"

Her eyes widened. I could see her swallow her emotions like she wasn't used to people being on her side, and it killed me all over again that a woman like her had ever felt alone in this world when I was there all along, waiting to stand by her side.

"Cool." She bumped his fist without even hesitating. "What?" She shrugged at me. "Why are you looking at me like that?"

"So this is a fun morning." I smiled over my cup of coffee, suddenly warm in my chest like my heart was happy, which was ridiculous. I'd always been happy.

Or at least I thought I was. Maybe I had been missing something. Joy.

Parker grabbed a banana and tossed it to me. "Remind you of something?"

Jagger caught it midair and dropped it immediately.

Parker winked. "I was just trying to lighten the mood. Who wants to go for a run?"

Jagger bit into his apple again. "I'm in, just gotta grab some shoes. Matt, you're a twelve, right?"

"Unbelievable," I grumbled. The guy used my stuff like it was his, asshole.

"You have seventeen pairs of running shoes, you'll survive." Jagger slapped me on the back. "Oh and bro, do you have a toothbrush?"

I glared. He was like Willow but male. Awesome, this should be great come Christmas, how had I never put two and two together? They were both annoying on purpose and too smart and talented, meaning they got away with everything. And I let them because I loved them both. Huh, maybe they did make sense after all.

"Kidding, I brought my own because I knew it was going to be a slumber party."

"Pain in my ass." I leaned against the counter, and just like it was normal, Parker walked over to me and I gathered her in my arms and kissed her cheek. "Run?"

"Yeah, I feel sore."

Willow snorted.

"In my legs, you dirty whore!" Parker responded without even looking at my sister, then lowered her voice. "And other places."

I choked on my next sip of coffee as she leaned up on tiptoes and licked the outside of my ear, sending all my blood south, and then whispered, "Tonight I think you should tie me up—with the whistle cord."

"Fuck." I locked eyes with her. "You're going to be a handful, aren't you? Am I going to need aspirin every night?"

"Weekly massages will help." She patted my back.

I rolled my eyes. "Dick massages, you mean?"

"Very funny." She slapped my ass. "Go get dressed, I want you to stretch me later."

"Funny, I thought I was the coach."

"And agent." She winked. "Don't forget."

She practically skipped out of the room, leaving me and Willow alone.

"So . . ." Willow licked her lips like she wasn't sure if she should bring something up.

"Spit it out, Willow."

"While I'm super excited you guys are together"—she cleared her throat and shifted on her feet a bit—"you do have a clause in your contract about dating clients . . ." She shrugged. "I can look past it, but . . ."

"Shit." I ran my free hand through my hair, frustrated that I hadn't thought of it and irritated that it was even an issue. I'd been so worried about how dating her would look to others that I hadn't even considered the legal ramifications. "I'll figure something out, maybe I can give her to another one of the—"

Willow shook her head. "But she trusts you. Look, it's not a big deal now, but once she inks a deal, which we know she will, she's going to need to separate business and personal. Wow, I just sounded so ridiculously old, like you, that I may need to buy a pair of spectacles, but the cute ones you get at Barney's that just make you look smarter."

My smile was strained as all the possibilities weighed my shoulders down. "You are smart."

"I know that," she said without sarcasm. "But thank you anyway. Just focus on your run and I'll go look through the contract. It's going to be fine, okay?"

"Okay." I kissed her forehead. "Promise me that you're happy with Jagger? I mean he's . . ."

"A total player, douche, and all-around pain in your ass, yeah, I get it, but he's incredible to me. I really, really like him, so don't mess this up just because you can't stand the fact that he saw me naked and we played tag . . . with whipped cream and Skittles."

I nodded. "Wow, and with that visual . . ."

"I was it." She laughed and did a little dance.

"Never again. We're never speaking of this again." I shuddered and walked off, thoughts of my business relationship with Parker plaguing my mind.

Chapter Twenty-Seven

PARKER

"You know . . ." I grabbed a bottle of water while Willow typed away on her laptop. The run had done wonders for my nerves. Matt had disappeared into his office and Jagger followed. "You could have told me your evil plan."

She grinned at the screen. "You guys would have fought it. I mean let's be honest, you already tried to fight it. I figured if I let you in on my evil plan you guys would kill each other first."

I shrugged. "You may have a point there."

"I know my brother, and I know you. Both so stubborn it's ridiculous but the best people I've ever known." More typing and clicking filled the room. She was working really hard for a Saturday. "Besides, I wasn't even sure it would work. It was hard enough lying about the hotel and pretending that I didn't notice all his lingering glances at your ass."

"I didn't linger on her ass," Matt said, sweeping into the room. Dark skinny jeans hugged his legs, perfectly complementing his brown boots and a tight green vintage tee that made him look like he was ready to go on tour somewhere.

I let out a girly sigh when he smiled my way, his glossy blond hair was seriously too thick and pretty. It wasn't fair.

I mean I was the girl who carried Pringles in her hair.

With the guy who could grace magazine covers and star in the next box-office blockbuster.

"Any luck?" He pointed the question to Willow.

"Nope." She sighed. "But I'll figure it out. Alright you two, just go have fun."

"We two?" I asked. "What are we two doing?"

Matt grinned and reached for my hands, interlocking our fingers as he pulled me into his arms. "I know you're stressed, I figured this would be the easiest way to get you to stop thinking."

"There's a lot of ways to get me to stop thinking."

"Sitting right here," Willow said in a singsong voice.

I ignored her and focused on his perfect lips as he flashed me a million-dollar grin.

"Dinner."

My stomach dropped. "Oh, so dinner as . . . agent and . . . gotcha. No, that would make sense, people wouldn't speculate—"

"Parker . . ."

"Yeah?" I pasted a happy smile on my face.

"We'll have the whole restaurant to ourselves."

"People, they . . ." My smile was so wide it was almost embarrassing. "They do those things?"

"My brother does those things. He has money to burn," Willow piped up. "Why do you think I have a shoe obsession?"

"What should I wear?" I bit down on my lip in excitement.

"Nothing." His first answer.

Another gag from Willow.

After a moment, he relented. "Just dress comfortable, alright? Nothing too fancy, I promise, just a nice dinner by the water . . ."

"Water?" I sighed happily. "Give me ten minutes."

I was not five steps down the hall when Willow followed me, dragged me into one of the guest rooms, and shut the door. "You're not wearing jeans."

"But—"

"I did not work my ass off to get you guys together for you to go out on your first real date with my brother in jeans."

I pouted. "He said comfortable."

"He's a guy, all he cares is if he can cop a feel later. You could wear a muumuu, and he'd be all, 'Oh, Parker, you're so beautiful, Parker, is that a chip in your hair, Parker? I love chips! Let's have a billion babies.'"

I gave her the finger.

She waved me off and pulled something black from yet another shopping bag scattered around the house; she was like the Easter bunny of fashion and gifts. "You'll wear this, with gold hoop earrings and my gold flats, and you're going to put on some makeup, not a lot, just some."

Twenty, not ten, minutes later, I was standing in the living room in a chic black jumpsuit with a plunging neckline. My hair was half up, and I'd let Willow put enough makeup on me to bring out my brown eyes and my tan skin. The gloss she gave me tasted like coconut, so that was a win.

"Here." She thrust a Louis Vuitton clutch at me. "And don't worry, I added condoms."

She just happened to say that when Matt walked in and nearly ran into a wall. I wasn't sure if it was because of the condom comment or because of the way I was dressed. Maybe both?

He cleared his throat.

I smiled, took the purse, and when Willow wouldn't let me go, I batted her away with said purse, grabbed my phone, and all but leaped into Matt's arms.

"You kids have fun!"

"Bye, guys!" Jagger rounded the corner with a bottle of wine. He was still here? Had the guy even left?

"Bastard better keep his hands to himself," Matt grumbled.

"I don't think it's his hands you're worried about," I said as I turned back to see Jagger devour Willow whole.

Damn, talk about aggressive on and off the field.

Maybe it was an athlete thing.

"So, look." I took a deep breath as we went outside, and Matt opened the car door for me. "I just—I wanted you to know that I would never trap a guy or lie to him. I'm on the pill, so—"

"Parker."

"And I'm really sorry. I wasn't thinking, I just . . . maybe that's my immaturity or my inexperience speaking. I mean before you, there was, well, we talked about that and then one other guy I dated for like six months, and then—"

"Parker."

"I don't know, it didn't even mean anything, we just got caught up and . . . oh God, now I sound like those commercials they make you watch in high school health class!" I pinched my nose and then chanced a look at a smirking Matt. "What? Why are you laughing?"

"Because I was going to apologize to you. I saw your blood test, your entire physical, I know you're on the pill, I know you're clean. I honestly didn't even think about it because I already knew, but you didn't know that about me, so I'm the one who's sorry. For the record, I haven't been with anyone in over a year."

"One. Year?" Why did that make me so happy? "As in three hundred and sixty-five days?"

"Yeah, let's not yell it, though . . ." He started the car and backed out. "But I would like to talk about the fact that you were with what sounded like one boyfriend in college and then . . ."

My stomach heaved. "Yeah."

"That should tell you one thing right there, Parker. It's not like you were this experienced seductress out to make a name for yourself. You didn't seduce him, you were afraid, he abused that power, that fear, and he was wrong, not you."

My throat closed up, tightened to a painful degree. "I just . . . I don't want to talk about it, not here, not now."

"We have to talk about it sometime, Parker. We have to discuss what you want to do."

I jerked my head to attention. "What do you mean? I would never play for LA. And as for Erik . . ."

"I know, which is why I called them this morning and said thanks but no thanks. That's what I'm talking about." He pulled onto the freeway toward downtown. "I just don't think you're ever going to have closure unless you come forward."

"No." I crossed my arms. "What if nobody believes me? What if someone finds out about us and uses it as a way to prove that I sleep around for my career? You would be ruined, I'd be done for, and all because he's a horrible human being!"

Silence.

I hated it when he was silent.

Because it said more than words did, didn't it?

"You're worth that risk to me, but you have to think about you right now, and know I am fully on board with Team Parker. I like her, I want her to succeed, I want her to have everything even if it means she doesn't have me," he finally said, putting his hand on my knee. "And you're right. We won't talk about it tonight. But the minute you make that Seattle team, I want to sit down with you and discuss it."

I wanted to shove his hand away and yell at him that I felt more for him than soccer . . . than anything. That nobody had ever loved me that much or even said words like that out loud. Tears filled my eyes; he was too much and yet everything I needed all at once.

"How is this going to work? You just put on your agent hat and during meetings I can't kiss you?"

He let out a sigh. "I'm in the same boat you are, just living day by day and wondering if I'm doing the right thing, especially since my heart keeps trying to speak before my head has a chance."

I smiled through my tears. "It's going to be okay, though, right?"

More silence, and then he picked up my hand and kissed the back of it. "I promise."

Why didn't I believe him?

And why did it seem like he didn't even believe himself?

Chapter Twenty-Eight

MATT

She was distant all night.

And I knew why.

I just wished I knew how to fix it.

We talked, we laughed, we did what we always did when we were together, which meant a lot of laughing, teasing, banter, but I could feel her pulling away, like she was already preparing herself for the worst.

We were at one of my favorite restaurants on the pier, and since I knew the owner and paid him to close it down for two hours, he was more than happy to take my money and let us have our privacy. But the food felt heavy in my stomach.

I poured her a small glass of wine, careful to monitor her alcohol, and then wanted to slap myself. At that moment . . .

I wasn't her dad.

I wasn't her coach.

I wasn't her agent.

And yet I felt like I had to wear all those hats for her. It was confusing even for me, because I'd never crossed that professional line with anyone, and now I wasn't sure how to proceed. How do you go from treating someone like a client to someone you could actually picture your life with?

"I don't want to lose you as a client," I said once the dessert menus were brought to our table.

Parker looked up, her eyes filled with sadness. "I don't want that either." Her smile fell. "Were you going to follow that up with a 'but'?"

"Maybe."

"I don't like buts."

"I love yours, but I prefer the term *ass*," I teased.

Her mouth twitched like she wanted to laugh. Shit. She was sexy.

"Look." I leaned forward. "I like you, I care about you, and when you care about someone you want to take care of them. I just don't know how to do that without ruining what we have. I don't know how to be the bossy agent but also be your boyfriend."

Her eyes widened. "Is that what you want?"

"To be your bossy agent and boyfriend?"

She nodded.

I exhaled slowly as I took in her pretty lips and the way her wide eyes locked onto every single movement I made. She was so pretty with her big, wide brown eyes. I just wanted to pull her into my arms and kiss her soundly, lie to her that it was all going to be fine, when the future was still so uncertain. "I want to be your boyfriend more."

Her smile was real then. "If I got to choose, I'd choose boyfriend too."

"So . . ." I reached my hand across the table. The candle flickered in the breeze from the ocean filtering through the window. "I'll figure out what to do about our contract. I'll find you someone that you can trust, someone that I can trust. How does that sound?"

"Like they won't take twenty percent?" she teased.

I kissed the back of her hand. "Hilarious, and you know I wouldn't even take a percentage from you, and that's the problem . . . We made it personal and that's not fair to either of us, it's hard to figure out where agent-client begins and being lovers ends."

"I know. I hate that you're right. But it feels like we're breaking up."

It was my turn to laugh. "I'm glad you're that emotionally attached to your agent."

Her voice lowered as she looked down at our joined hands. "Because he promised me everything—and he gave me more."

I was on her side of the table in seconds, my mouth caressing hers, her pliant lips opened to me as I slid my tongue past her lower lip, tasting the wine on her tongue and searching for more.

"Dessert?" I asked once we broke apart.

"Why yes, thank you for asking." She tilted her head, flicked my tongue with hers, and moaned into my mouth like she was starving for me. I couldn't get enough of her, of the way we fit together.

The waiter cleared his throat. "Did you need more time?"

"Dessert to go," I said without looking at him. "Two chocolate soufflés."

Parker cleared her throat.

"And vanilla ice cream," I added with an eye roll.

She grinned and pressed a kiss to my cheek. "It's like you read my mind."

"Yeah, it had nothing to do with the fact that you were pointing at the menu and giving me a death glare."

"None at all!" She laughed and then sobered. "As long as we're together, it's going to be okay."

"Of course it will." I kissed her again just as guests started filling the restaurant. The sadness on her face was like a kick to the gut.

I didn't want the secrecy any more than she did.

And when people looked over at us, paranoia struck. Did they know who I was? Who she was? Did they see the slight age difference that resembled her and her coach? Did it matter? To me she looked like a girl in her midtwenties, and I'd like to think I looked the same age.

My eyes darted left to right and back again as I tried to find a logical reason why it felt like we were being watched.

"Here you go, Mr. Kingston." The waiter handed me our dessert. "As always, thank you for visiting Elliot's."

"Course." I signed the bill and stood as Parker grabbed her purse. Her lips looked swollen, her hair tousled.

I led her out of the restaurant, my hand on her lower back as we left through the front doors and walked slowly to my car.

Parker gasped while I grabbed my key from my pocket.

"What? What's wrong?"

She pointed.

My luxury Porsche had key scratches down the passenger side, and on the window in bold letters it read WHORE.

"Come here." I pulled Parker into my arms and then searched for my phone.

"Willow," I barked. "Send a car to the restaurant and get me the chief of police. My car's been damaged, and it looks like someone is trying to send a threatening message."

Parker ducked her head against my chest. "You know the chief of police?"

Her teeth were chattering. Damn it. She was trying to be strong, but she didn't have to be anymore.

Not now.

"He's a family friend," was all I said, leaving out minor details such as the guy had been linked to the Italian mafia and had connections all over the world, mainly Sicily and Chicago. Whenever I asked him anything to do with his business dealings, he just gave me a blank stare and asked about soccer. Huge fan.

Within five minutes, which seemed quick even for Chief Johnny Alfero, a black SUV pulled up, followed by two police cruisers.

"Matt." Johnny got out of the SUV and held out his hand. "I'm sorry to be seeing you under such odd circumstances. I did a little homework on the way over. We haven't had reports of vandalism in the area and no record of any car burglaries in the past two weeks."

I sighed. "I think it's personal."

His dark eyebrows arched as I nodded to Parker.

"Personal," he repeated. "In what way?"

"Parker," I urged. "You can trust him."

Her face paled as she swayed in my arms like her legs couldn't hold her up anymore. "I can't."

"Parker, this could be your life. We don't know who did this, but it can't be a coincidence. If it's him . . ."

"He lives in LA!" She jerked away from me. "I just want to go home."

"Parker—"

"I need you to be my agent right now. I need you to be someone other than my caring boyfriend who wants me to tell a complete stranger about my past. Please." Tears spilled down her cheeks. "Please."

My heart cracked at her expression. I hung my head. "Okay."

Johnny put his hand on my back. "Why don't you take her home? I'll call you if anything comes up. We already have a tow truck coming to take your car to one of the auto-body shops. I'll text you the location?"

"Great."

"And you . . ." He turned his massive six-foot-four frame toward Parker. His blue eyes were so bright it was rumored that his superpower was reflecting the ocean's depths in them (that, according to Willow, was mainly from every female he encountered). "I want you to take my card." He pulled it out. "If you need anything, you call this number. It's private. And if you want to talk"—he nodded—"I can talk too. Sometimes it's easier to talk to someone that isn't friends or family. And if I need to bury a body"—he flashed a grin—"I know people."

She smiled.

I didn't.

Guy wasn't kidding.

I shook his hand again. "Thank you."

"Don't mention it." He nodded seriously as if he really didn't want us to mention it.

The town car arrived about thirty seconds later. I helped Parker into the seat, buckled her in, and then pulled her to my side once the car was back on the freeway.

Next to me, she stiffened.

"You're angry." I hated the helplessness I felt in my gut. I'd missed all of the signs because my focus was on the psychopath who did this and not on her.

"I told you I didn't want to talk about it, and then you said we wouldn't, and then that happens and . . ." She pulled away from me. "What part of 'I don't want to talk about it to anyone' don't you understand?"

"I understand all of it," I said, teeth clenched. "I understand that a crazy guy could be after you just because you made him look like an idiot. Yes, it could be coincidence, but I think both of us know it's most likely not. It was on your side of the car, like someone was watching us. And it was my car! The fact that he's been sending threatening letters, watching us, I don't know . . ."

Tears spilled over her cheeks. "I can't talk about it right now. Let's just . . ." She squeezed her eyes shut and reached for my hand. "Let me get through tryouts and then we can discuss it."

I kissed her fingertips. "Okay."

She sighed against my chest.

And a part of my heart righted itself again.

Until we pulled up to my house.

And saw the same word.

Spray-painted across my front door.

WHORE.

Chapter Twenty-Nine

PARKER

"Sleep." Matt kissed my forehead, but I was wide awake, stupefied into disbelief. Would Erik actually do something like that? Had he been following us? He seemed the most likely suspect, and the fact that anyone had been watching our home freaked me out.

Our home.

My safe place with Matt.

Someone threatened it, and I wanted to threaten them right back.

I hugged the pillow to my chest while Matt paced. He was like this shirtless, angry Greek god wearing a hole in the ground.

"I can't sleep if you don't sleep," I said with a sigh. "Plus you promised me dessert."

He looked up, concern and maybe a little bit of fear lined his face. "I'll hire security."

"Why would I need security when I have you?" I said in a dumbfounded voice.

"You'll be traveling with the team. I can't be there twenty-four seven, so yeah, I'm going to hire a giant to just stand over you so nobody can hurt you."

"First off . . ." My heart swelled at the gesture. Oh good, he was back to pacing again. "That's really creepy, someone should never just stand over another human. It's weird, and how would you get your vitamin D? Second, you can't protect me. If there's one thing I've learned in my past, it's that there comes a point when you need to learn how to protect yourself." My throat went dry. "I didn't. I chose the easy way out by not saying anything and then got violent when it ended up not being easy."

"You were terrified," Matt said in a soft voice.

"I didn't know what he was capable of then. He was just an arrogant coach with a god complex."

Matt tilted his head. "How did he handle rejection from other girls?"

"I don't think he did, I mean I don't think he ever got rejected by the girls I knew about, and we don't know anyone ever turned him down. For all I know he loved the attention and was pissed because I wasn't like them."

"So there could still be other girls suffering like you are," Matt argued.

"Can we not talk about Erik in our bed?"

Matt's lips twitched. "One night and now you're claiming it?"

"Why not? It comes with you, doesn't it?"

"Not exactly with me, but it's present when coming happens." He winked.

I rolled my eyes and burst out laughing.

"There it is." Matt sobered as he crawled onto the bed and pulled me into his arms. "There's my Cheetah Girl."

I slumped against him. "What if this gets in my head, messes up my tryout and—"

"Son of a bitch, that's it!" Matt yelled, scaring the ever-loving hell out of me.

"What? What's it?" I pressed a hand to my chest, my heart beating like crazy. The guy had a death wish. Next time I was going to punch him in the jugular.

"He's trying to get in your head." Matt grabbed my hands. "Maybe it triggered something when we turned down LA. Say the worst happens and the Reign passes, say other teams pass, say the only team left is LA . . ."

My stomach dropped as a wave of nausea rolled through my system. "Then what? Is he going to stop threatening me with name-calling? Is it going to turn into something more physical? Drastic?"

I stared down at the remote by the nightstand.

Matt pulled it away before I could grab it. "Don't. Even if he did the worst, even if he went to the media, what's the worst that could happen?"

"Oh, you know"—tears filled my eyes—"I get called a whore by complete strangers and the guy that hit me, and tried to rape me . . ." The minute the words left me, something snapped. I gasped and covered my mouth with my hands. Pain pounded through my body as I remembered the rest of that night, the words he said, the way I felt like I gave in.

The pop of his peppermint gum. "You want this, you know you want this."

"I don't want this," I remember saying. "Please, no . . ."

"Just enjoy yourself, we'll be so good together, just tell me which team you want and I'll get you in once I'm in . . ." He smirked at his own joke.

"Erik—"

"Say my name again, I like it, tell me to fuck you."

My clothes were gone. Where were my clothes?

Frozen, I squeezed my eyes shut as he pressed me against the wall, and then bent me over the training table. "Say you want it."

"No."

"Say it!" He pulled my loose hair so tight that I screamed. "Oh yeah, just like that . . ."

"I want it," I said through sobs. "I want it . . ."

I crumpled against Matt's chest, weeping. It was the missing piece, always the missing piece as I remember just leaving my body and letting it happen. I always remembered saying I wanted it.

Not because I did.

But because he forced me to.

Because he was hurting me.

Because I was afraid.

"Just cry." Matt held my sobbing body close. "It's okay, I'm not leaving, Parker. It's okay, just cry."

I wasn't even breathing as I tore angrily at my own clothes, they were suffocating me just like he had suffocated me.

Matt didn't even blink. He pulled my shirt over my head and then pulled the sheets away from my legs.

"He doesn't get this, Parker," Matt said softly. I started to hiccup. "He doesn't get our bed, our home, he doesn't get to steal this from us, alright?"

I nodded, crying so much that tears streamed down my body.

Matt pulled me back into his arms and rocked me until I cried myself out, until I nearly fell asleep.

He rocked me, and when he laid me down against the mattress and tucked me against his body, he whispered, "I love you . . ."

Chapter Thirty

Matt

I was more nervous than Parker, slept like shit, kept asking her if she was okay every few seconds, and somehow she looked better than I did, fresher, happier. How was that possible?

I wanted to sleep with a gun in case that fucker decided to come back to our house and then knew I'd end up in prison because I wouldn't just fire a warning shot.

No, I'd fire several shots directly into his pathetic dick and then see if I could take his head off.

I was livid.

I wanted to go to the media.

I wanted *her* to go to the media.

But first we had the tryout, and I promised her we wouldn't take any action until it was over.

I ran my hands through my hair and checked my Rolex again as a few other girls also trying to make the team ran around the field.

"She's going to do great." Slade popped a piece of gum in his mouth. "Trust me, she's talented. She's got this."

Jagger crossed his arms. "She just needs to focus on her footwork and make sure that the other girls don't shove her around."

"She's good at being bossy." I wiped my face with my hands. "Shit, I don't know if I can watch. Last night wasn't good, guys. I just . . . What if he's in her head?"

"No room for that, bro, not when you're in her heart." Jagger elbowed me.

Slade and I looked over at him.

"What?" He shrugged. "I can be sensitive."

I narrowed my eyes. "Just how sensitive are you around my sister?"

His lips twitched while Slade bit back a curse.

"Yeah, fantastic," I grumbled. Jagger smiled and looked away because he knew I wouldn't like his smug expression.

"Is this serious?" I found myself asking as tryouts started. Different girls ran to different stations, there was a staff member at each station. Shit, they had her doing passing drills first.

I would have preferred her in front of the goal, but passing was fine.

"I'm going to marry her," Jagger announced.

I cranked my head toward him. "The hell?"

"Your sister." His grin turned soft. "I mean she's too young right now, so I'm going to let her sow whatever oats she wants—but in the end, she'll choose me."

"Isn't she already sowing her oats?" Slade just had to ask, making me think about oats and Jagger and her and that damn game of tag again. "With dickhead here?"

I groaned into my hands. "How's Parker doing?"

"Are you seriously not watching? Where's the giant camera? Sign? The Capri Suns and orange slices? You're worse than a soccer mom taking her kid's Ritalin," Slade joked. "And she's consistent, which is more than I could say for number two, who keeps passing too far ahead, making her partner sprint to stop the ball."

I eyed the field with an intensity that almost seemed foreign. As if it was my team, I was coaching, and we were one game away from the playoffs. I exhaled and took another deep breath as one of the coaching staff blew his whistle and made a motion with his hand.

Parker moved to the other side of the field and played one-on-one defense against another team member. I grinned because this was where she outshined everyone else. She knew how to score, she knew how to pass, she had impeccable footwork and a great attitude when she wasn't scowling. But her ability to read plays was outstanding. It was one of the first things I had noticed when I watched her old tape.

"Left, right, left," I whispered under my breath. "Don't let her fake it, she's going left again."

And like she'd heard my words, Parker lunged to the left, stealing the ball from around the other player's legs and moving down the field. She stopped and kicked the ball back for another drill.

I clapped.

And suddenly wished I did have a sign and a video camera so I could remember this moment and show her how proud I was—how proud I *am*.

"Attagirl." Jagger clapped his hands and whistled. "She just handed that girl her ass."

I grinned with pride. "Yeah, she did."

"She still has to make it through the next few drills," Slade said, deflating my enthusiasm and pumping worry back into my veins. "She'll be fine. She just needs to stay focused."

My body tensed with each move she made as if I was the one doing it. On the outside, I was calm; on the inside, I was on that field with her, I was coaching her, encouraging her, berating her when she went the wrong way, and then blowing the shit out of my whistle when I needed her to hustle.

"No offense, Matt, but I've never seen a guy flinch so much in my entire life." Slade laughed. "You look like one of those dance moms who memorized their kid's entire routine and can't help but do some of those moves in the crowd."

Jagger burst out laughing. "Finally, a perfect nickname for him: Dance Mom Matt!"

They both fell into fits of laughter.

I ignored them.

Because she had one drill left.

Which some may think was the easiest.

Score as many goals as you can in under a minute.

Soccer balls stretched from one edge of the field to the other, each one lined up to a different shot she could strike from. She'd have to start at one end and kick them in order.

I flinched when the whistle blew.

And almost laughed when Jagger seemed to hold his breath while Slade pulled out his phone.

At least one of us was smart enough to document it.

The first kick was a bit wide but made it in, and as she went down the line, the kicks got tighter and tighter until she drilled one straight down the middle that had the goalie stumbling backward as the ball hit the net.

I grabbed Slade's arm and Jagger's shirt.

We waited like that, holding our breath.

And then Parker looked over her shoulder to me, blew a kiss, turned, and drilled her last goal into the corner of the net.

"YES!" I jumped into the air, and Slade and Jagger shook me.

We were celebrating, and she hadn't even made it yet.

But we knew soccer.

We knew the game.

The coaching staff couldn't stop smiling.

And I knew Parker was one of the main reasons.

We hung back until the final girl went. I waited for Parker, she ran toward me at full speed.

I couldn't help but catch her in my arms, and the need to kiss her was so desperate I almost did it in front of everyone.

My eyes fell to her lips. "In my mind I'm kissing the hell out of you right now and already at work stripping that sweaty uniform from your body. I'm telling you how fucking fantastic you are, and I'm swearing I'll prove to you just how proud I am by worshipping every inch of your body."

Her eyes went wide. "Is there a reason we're still here, then? Because that sounds way better than ice cream for a job well done."

"We can do that too." I chuckled, swinging her around and then setting her down on her feet just as Slade and Jagger walked up and gave her hugs and high fives.

"What do you think, boys? Should I play for the men's team instead and help you win another championship?"

Slade choked out a laugh. "Yeah, maybe one day you'll get there."

"Small fry," Jagger joked.

She stuck out her tongue at both of them just as the head coach, Darius Peters, approached us.

"Who do I have to thank for getting Parker ready for tryouts? I wanna give him or her a call." Darius grinned from ear to ear.

"Actually," I chuckled, "that would be me."

Darius's eyebrows shot up. "Thought you retired."

"It turns out I had a little left to give, plus I had a shiny new whistle I wanted to use."

"Ah . . ." He laughed. "And you two?" He looked at Slade and Jagger.

"Oh, we helped kick her ass the other day in a scrimmage," Jagger said with laughter in his voice. "But she ended up handing us ours."

"Speak for yourself." Slade shoved him with a grin.

Darius was already looking at Parker with the word *championship* in his eyes. "I'm glad we didn't pass on you, Parker. You'll be hearing from us soon, alright?"

Parker nodded excitedly, I could tell she was trying not to scream and dance around us. But she remained professional.

Until we got back to the Benz, about a half hour later.

Then she was dancing in the car and starting to strip.

I about choked on my tongue when her shirt went flying. "Maybe let's wait until we're home for that."

"Home." She spread her arms wide and then seemed to deflate. "Home."

"Something wrong?"

"No, nothing, it's just . . ." She made a face. "It feels that way, to me at least."

"Good." I rubbed her leg, and when we pulled up to a stop sign, I couldn't help myself. I reached across the console and kissed her long and hard, so deep that I didn't want to come up for air, but the honking behind me was clue enough I couldn't handle myself in public.

I needed my girl in private.

"Yeah, yeah." I waved in the rearview mirror and took off with a half-naked Parker holding onto my hand and beaming like she'd just won the World Cup.

We wasted no time. I pulled into the garage, closed the door, and raced her through the house and into the bathroom.

"Are you hitting the showers with me, Coach?" She peeled her sports bra off her perfect little body.

"Sounds dirty . . ." I said in a low voice. "A bit wrong . . ."

"No." She smiled up at me as she helped me shrug down my jeans. "This isn't wrong, not you and me."

"No." I grinned. "Never."

She pressed an open-mouthed kiss to my lips and let out a giggle when I hooked my fingers in her shorts and wiggled them to the floor. I carefully discarded each cleat, sock, shin guard. And then it was just the smell of sweat, grass, and victory all wrapped up in one perfect package staring down at me like I was the reason for her happiness when she had no idea that she was the sole reason for mine.

Her hair was a tangled auburn mess at her shoulders, her eyes lit up when I ran my hands up her thighs and cupped her hips. "I'm so damn proud of you, Parker."

"Yeah?" She grinned, chewing on her lower lip as my hands caressed their way up her body until we were face to face.

"Yeah." I brushed a kiss on the corner of her mouth. "Oh, and I have a new nickname, Dance Mom Matt. Unfortunately, I think it's going to stick."

She made a face then burst out laughing. "Then where's my snack, bitch?"

"That's it!" I threw her over my shoulder and carried her into the small shower in the guest bathroom, wishing mine was remodeled so we could spread out and just camp in there for the next day, feeding each other grapes or whatever the hell you do as a happy couple.

"Sto-op." She laughed as water sprayed all over our faces, running down our bodies. "Okay, I'm sorry I called you a bitch, but I'll take my snack now, Coach." She dropped to her knees before I could stop her and then I was dying a slow death in the heat of her wicked mouth as I leaned against the shower tile so I wouldn't crush her with my weight or my enthusiasm as she worked her tongue around me.

"Parker." I ground out her name as I moved my hips. "Bend over . . . now."

"Wha—"

I had her on her feet, her back facing me within seconds. She panted my name as I cupped her breasts from behind, watched the water slide down her perfect ass. I rubbed the tender skin there. "This is mine . . ."

"Yes." She threw her head back.

"All of this." A wave of dangerous possession took hold as I jerked her against me, found her entrance, and sank in with one fluid thrust that had her wet hair slapping my chest as my hips moved with hers.

"Yes, yes," she panted. "Please, Matt, right there . . ."

"Where?" I joked, earning a helpless sigh from her as I angled my body and pulled her entire weight in the air. "Put your hands on the wall, yeah, like that . . . and your feet right on the ledge . . ." I nipped her ear. "And hold on tight."

With that angle I had gravity on my side and the fact that she was bent just enough for me to hit every deep and delicious spot that had her thighs pulsing and our bodies buzzing in ecstasy.

"Matt!" Her fingers clawed at the tile as I sent her over the edge only to dive in right after her.

Parker's body trembled with aftershocks as she slumped against me. I pulled out and then picked her up in my arms and kissed her chin, her mouth, her eyes. "So proud."

"We're not done, right?"

"Done?" I searched her eyes. "Parker, what's wrong?"

"You're done coaching me." She stared straight at my chest like she was afraid to look at me. "And you've admitted you need to find me a new agent, but . . ."

"MATT!" Willow roared, pounding urgently on the door. "I have an idea about this agent thing."

I let out a deep sigh. "Not now, Willow!"

"But I think that if you just . . . actually tell me yes or no."

"Yes?" I shook my head. "Can we do this later?"

"It's going to solve everything, just give me the go-ahead."

"Go away!" I gave Parker an apologetic look.

"So that means do it?" She knocked again.

"Yes, just go!" Good luck, Jagger. Good. Luck.

"Hey." I set Parker down on her feet. "Just tell me what's in your head right now."

"You." Her lower lip trembled. "You and soccer, sometimes tacos, and randomly I'll think about a pancake."

My lips twitched. "Really?"

"I don't want to be done. I don't want this to be done." She slid her hands down my chest.

"Parker, just because I'm not your coach doesn't mean we're suddenly done . . . this relationship wasn't based on any of my job titles, or the fact that you're an athlete."

Her eyes lit up as she met my gaze. "So you're saying . . ."

"I'm saying I'm not letting you go." I cupped her cheeks with my palms. "I'm saying that you're my girlfriend, that you're mine. That I'm not kicking you out just because you think that for some reason your worth and our identity as a couple are based on anything other than my desire to be with you because of you. And for the record, I don't give a fuck what people say, I just want you."

She nodded, her arms tangled around my neck so tight I almost couldn't breathe. "I needed to hear that."

"I'll tell you that every day until you believe me."

"I may need it every day."

My chest contracted as I let myself feel her body press against mine, let myself soar with the possibility that this was real and that nothing was going to stand in the way.

And just when I was getting comfortable with the idea that this could be our future, the ball dropped.

Because I'd completely forgotten it was hanging there in the first place.

Waiting to strike.

Waiting to destroy.

Chapter Thirty-One

PARKER

I was too excited to sleep that night.

I would get an offer this week, possibly even today, according to Matt.

The excitement was something tangible I could focus on. I knew I was already driving the entire household crazy. Every time I heard a cell phone ring I was ready to tackle the person answering it.

It just wasn't the good news.

It was news in general that didn't have to do with Erik or with the vandalism. It had been two days, and the police had nothing. At least it forced Matt to set up cameras around the house.

And that was the other annoying thing. Every time the Ring app went off on my phone, I jumped a foot. Apparently, it detected the slightest motion and picked up on everything from the UPS guy to a bird flying in front of the house. Needless to say, it made me feel both paranoid and oddly safe.

I flipped through a few more channels on the TV and checked my cell. It was nine a.m. the day after tryouts.

Nine a.m. and I was already driving everyone insane.

I clapped my hands in front of me, rolled my eyes, then reached for the remote again and flipped through the channels.

". . . developing story about a love affair gone wrong." The hair on the back of my neck stood on edge as I watched the news channel.

A girl about my age described how her doctor had touched her inappropriately. I recognized her as one of the elite ice skaters that had made it to the Olympics during the last trials. She was so pretty, young, successful, and already had her own Wheaties box.

And she didn't look like herself as she cried in front of the reporter. It was like she was watching someone else relay the story, like she was trying to separate herself from the actual attack. I knew that hollow feeling well. If you admitted it, it had happened. A picture flashed of the team doctor. He was young, attractive, and had been one of her personal physicians for four years.

And according to her, for four years he had taken advantage of her, molested her, and when she spoke up had countersued her for ruining his reputation.

According to him, she was angry he had refused to give her a cortisone shot, and because of that she blamed him for not getting a gold medal. "I would never put my license at risk—no matter who asked me," he said smugly to the camera as he left court. "No more questions."

My stomach dropped. This was me. I was watching my life through someone else's eyes, someone braver, someone willing to risk it all to protect those around her, willing to put her reputation on the line because wrong is wrong. No is no.

"Sources are confident this is going to be a long battle between the two, since Miss Davenport didn't come forward until recently, when allegations that the doctor had been mistreating other women were discovered."

I needed to do something.

Say something.

My body vibrated with rage.

My cell went off again.

Stupid Ring app.

I flipped off the TV.

My brain was going a million miles a minute. Was I just as bad as Erik? For not saying anything? For not going to the right people? I thought I had when I told my therapist, without realizing she was sleeping with Erik and had been for months.

I squeezed my eyes shut.

This was supposed to be a happy day.

A happy week.

And still, he haunted me.

Would it always be like this?

"Parker?" Matt's voice sounded different. I jerked my head in his direction and waited for the good news. Instead, he looked uneasy.

"I didn't make the team." I hung my head.

"No, I'm not sure about the team yet, but I did just get a phone call from Darius. He wanted to know if he could stop by and talk with you. I told him he was welcome to come. He was already in the car and should be here in five or ten minutes."

My chest felt heavy as I tried to read Matt's expression. "What aren't you telling me?"

He stared at me for a few brief minutes before saying, "He asked about our relationship."

"As in our working relationship?"

"As in our romantic relationship . . . he wanted to know if it was a trend . . ."

"If what was a trend?" I fired back. "What the hell are you talking about?"

"I don't know how he knows, Parker. God knows we were careful, but someone tipped him off about Erik. All he knows is that according to an unnamed source, you pursued your coach in order to further your own career—and all he knows from that same source is that you are living under my roof, under my care, while I coached you, and that last night we were seen at a stop light kissing, with you in nothing but your sports bra."

My mouth dropped open as terror threatened to split me in two. The very man I wanted—I *needed*—to tell me it was going to be okay was looking at me like it wasn't, like we couldn't come back from this. Like I never would.

"Matt . . ." I licked my dry lips. "I need you to be my agent now. Tell me what to do, how do I handle this?" Tears welled in my eyes as my throat got thick and heavy. "I don't know how to lie to him and I don't want to. I don't want to lie about us, but if I don't—"

"I get it," Matt said softly. "And I'm going to make it easy on you, Parker. Choose your dreams." He didn't touch me, didn't walk over to me and pull me into his arms. "I'm not the reason you're here, you're the reason you're here, your talent, your tenacity—it's you. Worry about you. Not me."

"But . . ."

He silenced me with a sad smile.

"That can't be the only option!" I jumped to my feet.

"It is the only option," Matt said through clenched teeth. "Right now you're just another one of my athletes ready to sign what should be a seven-figure deal with one of the best teams in the US. As your agent, it's my job to tell you that another option doesn't exist!"

"You mean we don't exist." I hung my head as a solitary tear dripped from my cheek onto the expensive concrete floor.

Matt braced my shoulders with his hands, his face filled with agony, his smile gone. "When he walks in that door, the only thing that matters is your soccer career."

I reached for him, fisted his shirt in my right hand, and pulled him close. "And when he walks out?"

Matt's eyes fell to my mouth. "I wish I knew."

The doorbell rang.

He crushed his mouth to mine then.

And I hated that kiss.

I hated it more than I hated anything.

Maybe even Erik.

Because it tasted like good-bye.

"I'll get it!" Willow yelled in her usual everyone-must-be-wearing-ear-plugs-so-I-need-to-double-the-effort fashion.

Matt hung his head, and we broke apart. I counted the seconds from the time his fingertips left my skin, from the moment he backed away, and then, when he left me standing in the foyer to greet the coach, I had to ask myself, Was this the most important dream I had?

Or had Matt given me another one?

I was too confused to think.

All I knew is I wanted both.

The man, the dream. They weren't complete without each other, I just didn't know how to have both while still protecting him, protecting us from my past, my reputation, without killing his and my future with my new team—that is, if they still wanted me.

"Parker!" Darius waltzed right in and shook my hand. "I hope you got some rest last night?"

My mind flashed to images of Matt and me in the shower, him licking down my neck, my hands pressed against the cold hard tile as he filled me, as we became whole and just stayed that way as water cascaded over our bodies.

"Yeah," I croaked. "I crashed pretty early."

Next to me, Matt didn't as much as smirk. He was back to being the asshole agent who'd screw his own grandma in order to ink a deal, wasn't he?

I thought that was what I needed.

What I wanted.

But now I knew the truth.

Behind all of the business was a man, a wonderful man who made me laugh, who held me when I cried, who helped me chase a dream

I wasn't sure I could still chase without getting laughed out of the stadium.

"Willow, why don't you grab some coffee?" Matt flashed his megawatt grin toward Darius. "So what would you like to officially discuss?"

Darius folded his hands as he sat, his cheeks pinked a bit, making me even more uncomfortable as I waited.

"It's none of my business, it really isn't." Darius cleared his throat a few times, then pulled off his ball cap, ran a hand through his thinning, buzzed gray hair then put it back on. "Someone called and said they saw you two kissing after tryouts. Normally that kind of thing is not any of our business, but they prefaced it with a story about your relationship with your coach in college." Darius cleared his throat. "This person said you were in a sexual relationship in hopes that he would help further your career."

My entire body stiffened.

"Again, this isn't any of my business. I was getting ready to offer you a starting position, but our club is newer than others. Our reputation banks on girls who are good role models, so I need to know that we have nothing to worry about."

I couldn't find my voice as Willow waltzed over and handed him a cup of coffee. "What are we talking about?"

"Um . . ." I shook my head. "Let me start with college . . . I was . . ." This was it, wasn't it? The crossroads people talk about. Where you're forced to do the right thing even though it feels wrong, like you're standing in front of a firing squad ready for the countdown to begin.

My heart thumped painfully against my ribs.

My body was sore.

My head hurt.

And then I opened my mouth and the words just came out. "I want to be a good role model. I just don't think I'm that person, at least not as I am sitting across from you right now. Because I kept a secret." Tears filled my eyes as Matt's stunned expression met mine, one of shock and then pure love as he nodded slowly. "I was raped by Erik Sluvan when I was twenty-two years old. He was my coach. He was an authority figure. I had no romantic relationship with him. No relationship whatsoever outside of being one of his star athletes. I punched him in the face because he punched me in mine when he tried to rape me. I punched him because he didn't understand the word no. And the only other person I've ever told is Matt, who's been trying to convince me to come forward. But I'm scared. I'm scared you're going to look at me as someone who's playing a victim." I found strength in my own voice even as my hands shook, as my body jerked forward. "I am a victim. I'm a victim of a man who would do anything to get what he wants and who preys on innocent women. He sent me to anger management after the first time, you know." I shook my head and stared down at my hands. "When I confided in the therapist about what happened, she told Erik everything. I later learned that they were sleeping together, so my complaint is not even in the school records, and according to everyone involved, I'm just an angry girl who got pissed at her coach and became a diva. I'm still angry, but I'm angry because if I cry anymore over this, I'm afraid it might break me. This isn't about soccer, Coach, this is about . . . someone helping me heal and fight for my dreams, the very dreams Erik tried to kill the minute he told me to take my clothes off."

Darius was very quiet.

He stared me down for longer than seemed necessary. And then he stood.

Was he just going to leave?

I stood with him, not sure what to do.

He pulled me into his arms and hugged me so tight I couldn't breathe. When he pulled away, he had tears in his eyes. "I have two daughters." He wiped at his eyes. "I'm going to tell you the same thing I would tell them."

I waited in tense silence.

"Next time go for the family jewels and kick them twice."

I exhaled in relief and laughed through my tears. "Yeah, I'll remember that."

"Practice starts next Monday, on one condition."

"Anything." Was this really happening? Was I not getting punished? Why was my head still so twisted that I thought I was the one that would get into trouble for his mistakes? I hated him. I hated him so much.

"You file a police report." He put his hand on my shoulder. "You file a police report so they can look into it. I doubt you were the first, or the last, Parker. Men like that, they don't just stop because someone punches them in the face on national TV, alright? I think this will not only help you move on, but help you save others. This is why you're going to be a leader, because you're going to do the hard thing. I need you to do the hard thing."

I took a shaky breath as respect for this man bombarded me from all sides. He was right. And suddenly Matt's words about men being men and not being like Erik hit me full force. They were both right. "Okay. I'll call the police. I'll file a report."

"Good girl." He winked. "I'll send the practice schedule over to your agent."

"You got my email." Matt held out his hand.

"Oh, actually"—Willow stood and grinned—"that would be my email. Because of the romantic relationship between these two we didn't feel it would be professional for Matt to continue representing Parker. She's officially my first client, but I look forward to many future dealings, Darius, and might I add, that is a fantastic jacket!"

"Oh . . ." He beamed. "Yes, well, the wife has good taste."

"In more ways than one." She winked.

I would have gagged at her flirting had I not been so shocked. I gawked at Matt, who looked just as stunned.

"Oh, and Darius"—Willow put her hand on his arm—"let me escort you out. I expect that the travel schedule will be accompanied by her signing bonus and details of her new contract?"

"Trained her well, Kingston." Darius barked out a laugh as they walked over to the door like I didn't just confess all of my dirty laundry to my future coach.

I'd had no other choice.

And instead of breaking down and sobbing against the nearest solid object—that being Matt—I smiled.

Once the door shut, it was Willow who was in tears. Willow who ran at me full speed, pulled me into her arms, and then shook me. "I would have killed him for you. I still can."

Mascara stained her cheeks. She tried to wipe it away, only to make it worse.

"Willow?" Matt cleared his throat. "What's this 'you're her agent' business?"

A grin stretched across her face. "You were in the shower. You gave me the go-ahead through the door. But I was ready to veto your vote because you were both naked, and I figured the only way for you guys to be together without speculation was for me to take her on, duh. It's like two and two. Peanut butter and jelly. Cake and milk—"

"We get it." Matt held up his hand. "But you realize that's not the only issue, right? She's a lot younger than me, and—"

I sucked in a sharp breath, suddenly hurt he would bring up another hurdle after all the healing and closure I'd just experienced. "Don't give me that look."

His tone was gentle. "Willow, give us a minute."

Willow nodded, still wiping at her face. Matt pulled me into his arms for a hug.

I clung to him and refused to let go.

"I'm so damn proud of you," he whispered against my hair. "So proud."

"Why do I feel like you're going to follow that up with a 'but'?"

"Parker . . ." He didn't pull away, just kept saying words against my neck, inhaling my hair like it made him both happy and sad. "I want this for you so bad. Seeing you sitting there, getting your dream handed to you—there's nothing like it. You still have so many good years of soccer ahead of you, of travel, of being a part of one of the best clubs in the world. I don't want *us* to be a hindrance. I don't want you to regret your soccer career in any way, and I don't want you to resent me either. I guess what I'm trying to say is that I know you're young and it's okay if you wake up tomorrow morning and decide that living on your own, controlling your own destiny after having your past control so much of your present, is what you need right now—it's okay. I won't like it, but I'll be okay."

I smiled against his chest. "Are you basically giving me a free pass right now? Like 'Oh, it's okay that you're going to break my heart and I'm going to break yours but it's cool because you're young and we have a few good years of sex'?"

"No," he grumbled. "Yes. Maybe?"

"You love me." I tightened my grip around his neck. You could have bounced a quarter off the muscles that tightened in his body. "It's okay, I know you do. Real love sacrifices or stupidly thinks that the only way to know if it's real is if you give it away, run away, fly, bird, fly . . . But, what if I want to be captured?"

"What bird wants to be captured?"

"One who has a fabulous boyfriend." I sighed and pulled away, looking into his beautiful eyes. "One who really likes the cage. One who gets to sleep naked and eat tacos off her boyfriend's six-pack—"

"We've never done that."

"Yet," I pointed out. "But I did just get signed to a professional team, so I'm thinking taco Tuesday on your six-pack is in our future."

"Only if I get to eat your taco—"

"GUYS!" Willow yelled from the other room. "Stop talking so loud, it's embarrassing, and frankly, I think the plant heard you. It just died."

I rolled my eyes and pressed a kiss to Matt's mouth. "I'm yours if you'll have me."

"I'll have my decision after taco Tuesday." He grinned against my lips and then deepened the kiss, his head angling as he gripped my ass.

And then another sigh from Matt.

"Stop that! You're ruining my happy!" I swatted him on the shoulder.

"I'm old." He hung his head.

"Wait, you've been spending weeks trying to convince us you're not old."

"To you, I'm old." He winced like it came out wrong. "I just, I guess this is my way of saying I want to protect you."

"Great." I parted his lips with my tongue and lingered there, tasting him, reveling in his perfect kiss, the faint smell of his skin. "Protect me by staying at my side and in my arms, not by leaving me."

He exhaled, dragging his mouth against mine, drugging me with his taste as he held me tight against him. "I can do that."

"So about those tacos . . ."

Chapter Thirty-Two

MATT

"At least let me drive you to practice." I crossed my arms while Parker ran around me and grabbed a banana then tried to pry open her shaker cup using one hand.

Sighing, I took it from her, filled it with ice and water, then grabbed two scoops of protein and dumped it in. "You get your extra water bottle?"

"Yeah, and the hydration supplements you ordered for me last week." She flashed me a wink, I tried not to gape but she was beautiful, mine. Clean skin, huge smile. Strong legs. Mine.

"Awesome. The extra pair of cleats is already in your bag, and I packed information about a few sponsorships for you to look over. Willow, in all her agent knowledge, said to give you time to adjust, but I pulled the boyfriend card and said I was excited to see who was interested. Then she wouldn't shut up about it. Remember, you can always say no." I turned to see Parker grinning at me from ear to ear. She was wearing a Seattle practice jersey, short black shorts, and knee-high socks. I wanted to strip her naked and beg her to stay home.

My home.

Our home.

We still hadn't discussed what would happen after the summer was over.

Would she move out and find her own place with Willow like they planned? Or would I just beg her to stay like I planned?

The prospect of not having her in the house felt like a kick in the gut. But Parker deserved this moment. It was her first practice, and I'd like to think that as her boyfriend I did even better than as her coach in getting her completely stretched out, sore in all the right places, and ready to go.

"Why are you smiling at me like that?" she asked, a little breathless like she could read my mind and all the dirty thoughts floating around in there.

I tossed her the protein shake and crossed my arms. So damn pretty.

Parker laughed. "You're cute when you're worried. You know that your vein's popped out again, right?"

I instantly touched the vein and then flipped her off. "Cute."

"Hey." She spread her arms wide. "You fell for it."

I tackle-hugged her and then swung her around, dangling the key fob to one of my five cars in front of her. "Don't tell Willow I let you take the Benz."

"I swear." She winked and reached for the fob.

I jerked it away. "No speeding."

"Are you my boyfriend or my dad?"

I pulled her against me so she could feel what she did to me, the heat of arousal even just standing next to her was almost painful. "I think you know the answer to that question."

She cupped me, and then bit down on my neck.

I growled and pushed her against the counter, capturing her mouth with mine and pressing the fob against her palm. "If you don't leave now, I'm going to be the one driving, and it won't be a car."

"Ah, good one." She slapped my ass and made her way around me, grabbing all her gear. "I'll call you when practice is done, okay?"

"Okay . . . and, Parker?" I hated ruining her day, but it needed to be addressed.

"Yeah?" She was halfway to the door.

"Johnny called. He said he's going to have everything set up at the house so you're more comfortable during the interview, alright?" I knew she hadn't forgotten about pressing charges, about telling her story. We'd both decided to let her have practice and one good day before all hell broke loose in the soccer world, and I was glad she agreed to talking about it along with Darius.

"I know." Her smile was strong. "I'm ready, Matt."

"You're so brave." I walked up to her and kissed her forehead. "Now, off you go . . ."

She laughed. "Don't follow me in the minivan, it's weird."

"You little shit." I shoved her toward the door. "Go be an ass to your new coach."

She disappeared then poked her head back out the door. "I want you to bring your whistle to bed."

"Go!" I laughed and shut the door and then made my way to my office, where Willow was currently camped in the corner like a college student surviving off air and caffeine. I had to hand it to her, she was working her ass off for Parker and already had two endorsements plus five sponsorships lined up.

One thing she inherited from me?

My ability to talk my way into and out of everything.

She charmed the shit out of everyone.

Jagger included.

I growled.

"Could you do that elsewhere? I'm busy over here." She typed away at her computer and then jumped to her feet, nearly knocking her coffee off the chair next to her. "Matt?"

"What?" I opened my laptop and put in my Bluetooth headset. "I have a conference call in ten."

"Erik stepped down as assistant coach for LA." She turned her computer to mine. "You think it has anything to do with Parker?"

Uneasiness washed over me. We were a few states away. It could be nothing. Then again, I thought back to the vandalism. But nothing had happened since then, and the police had arrested a few kids two days ago for vandalism. We suspected it was connected to the crime on my car, but we still had suspicions about who vandalized my front door. Who knew? Maybe I was just being stupid paranoid.

"Does it say why?" My eyes greedily searched the small print.

"Nope." She sighed. "But I can do a little research or even call down to the station."

"Yeah." I leaned forward. "Actually, could you give the coach, Billy, a call? At least introduce yourself then charm him to death and ask for more information?"

"On it." She flashed me a grin. "See? What would you do without me?"

"What, indeed," I grumbled, and then smiled when she wasn't looking. My annoying sister has saved me in more ways than one.

Damn it. I was going to have to give her a bonus, wasn't I?

Chapter Thirty-Three

PARKER

I was suddenly relieved Matt put me through hell because I was officially one of the only girls left standing at the end of day one.

"Good job, Parker." One of the new girls who'd just made the team, Eileen, gave me a high five and then winced. "My everything hurts."

"Hah, yeah, well, had I not gotten my ass kicked these last two weeks I'd be in the same boat, but as it is I think I have a tub of ice calling my name."

"Yeah." A shadow crossed her face.

"Whoa." I stopped her. "Are you okay?"

"Hmm?" She forced a smile. "No, yeah, totally, I just, sorry, my mind isn't really on soccer right now, I actually transferred from another team."

"How did I not know that?"

"They still made me try out to make sure I meshed well with the team, you know how they are. They want good character, teamwork, it's not a single-person sport."

I whistled. "No, it's not. No room for divas here."

Her smile was soft, sad but soft. "Yeah, well, you were really great. I'm going to go home."

I frowned. "You aren't going to hit the showers?"

Her pale face was back again. "No, I, um, actually have an appointment, so I'll just try not to scare them away with the sweat."

"Alright." I smiled warmly. "See ya!"

I followed the rest of the girls into the locker room, smiled and chatted with a few, and realized that even though they were my teammates, the only person I really wanted to talk to was Matt.

Maybe Eileen had the right idea?

I grabbed my gear, put on my black Nike jacket, and waved good-bye. Cell in hand, key fob zipped in my bag, I sprinted out on sore legs to the Benz.

The fact that I was even driving a car that cost more than my college tuition made my head spin.

But Matt made it feel normal.

Like it was just a car.

It was just life.

And he didn't live it as if the world owed him anything. He worked his ass off, which just made me love him even more.

I stopped running.

Love.

I'd been saying it in my head for weeks, which sounded stupid, but I just, I didn't want him to think that I was saying it to him because I was infatuated or I didn't know my own mind.

As much as we joked about it, I was well aware that I was only twenty-two turning twenty-three in a few short months.

I knew our age difference.

But part of me felt like I'd been forced to grow up on my own, with a dad who didn't care, and no family to speak of.

I sighed and went to open the back door, shoved my duffel in, and then grabbed my phone to text Matt.

Once I got in the car I began to type out a message: Headed ho

"You look good." Erik's voice came from behind me.

I reached for the driver's door as he grabbed ahold of my jacket. Panic hit me like a wave of nausea as I struck him with my phone then fumbled with the door handle, but his hand remained on the neck of my jacket. The door flung open and I leaped out of the car and out of my jacket, leaving it clutched in his hands.

Pulse pounding, I ran as fast and hard as I could back to the stadium. People! I needed to be around people. He cared too much about appearances; he would never do anything around other people. I pulled open the stadium door with him running close behind.

I rounded a corner and saw the coach's office. When I tried the door, it was locked.

I kept running. Should I try the girls' locker room? Could we all fight him off?

He grabbed for my shoulder, but I elbowed him and kept running. I decided to head to the field. There were definitely people there. I ran toward the middle, where there were two members of the coaching staff.

"Stop!" I yelled, holding my hands up and away from him.

"Stop?" He spread his arms wide. "Stop what? This is your fault! All of it! You were supposed to sign with LA, not Seattle!"

I stared at him dumbfounded. "Are you insane? Why would I ever want to be near you after what you did to me!"

He rolled his eyes. "Same old story, I guess. Playing the victim like always," he scoffed while I fought for my next breath and prayed that someone would save me. He was a monster and I was his victim, and I knew by the look in his eyes he wouldn't stop. My breath came in short bursts, like I couldn't suck in enough air to save my life. Anger pulsed like a heartbeat against my skin. I was so angry, so done with him, yet so afraid at the same time. I needed him to talk, to confess, long enough that someone would hear or see that I was in trouble. "Okay, I'll play along, I hurt you, and you screamed in pleasure, does that sound about right?"

My stomach heaved as I fought to keep down its contents. He twisted everything. He was delusional! "Get help!" I yelled at one of the assistants out of desperation. Bye, Matt, bye, soccer life. It didn't matter, suddenly the only thing that mattered was getting help and getting him away from innocent people. "Call the police, now!"

The assistant pulled out his cell at about the same time Erik pulled out a gun. "I wouldn't do that if I were you."

"Erik, put the gun away," a strong voice said. It was me, my voice. Was I actually standing in front of a man with a gun and telling him to put it away?

"No, you see, this wasn't part of the plan, Parker. The plan was us. Together. Your future was us!" He waved the gun around. "You were the only one who said no! Who had the balls to look at me and say no! Do you realize what that does to a man? I could have made you great! I was everything to you! I saw the hero worship in your eyes, and then nothing!"

My eyes widened. "Erik, you were my coach, nothing more. You took advantage of me. Who knows who else you took advantage of!"

"They were never you. There's something so sweet about rejection, about the chase," he said in a pitiful voice. "It was always about you, about us, about your shining career and me as your mentor. You never gave me what I needed, I asked again and again, and after once you just shut down, you rejected me, so now I'm going to reject you . . ." His gun slowly moved from the assistant to me. "You fucking left me!"

"Because you raped me!" I screamed. "You're sick, you need help!"

His eyes turned cold. "Is it wrong to love you? To love your talent? To want to spend my life with someone who loves me just as much? I know how you feel about me. Those smiles you sent my way. The provocative clothing you wore to get my attention. The times you looked at me while you showered. I watched you, you know. I watched you every day after practice, when you would close your eyes and moan my name."

I choked back the urge to hurl as I remembered all those days I thought I heard someone in the locker room and nobody was there. The lonely nights I practiced on my own and thought my imagination was getting the best of me. All the times I asked my coach, who I trusted, to stay outside and walk me to my car because I was scared.

The very coach who was a predator.

Who raped me when I trusted him most.

Erik's hand started to shake.

Either he was having second thoughts or I had an opening to try to fight him. Adrenaline pumped through my body as I walked toward him. "Is that why you left the university?"

"I left because some little snitch told the athletic director about the allegations!" Shit, they finally did something? When I was gone? Really?

"It wasn't me," I lied. "I would never do that to you."

"You're a whore!" he roared. "You don't deserve me."

"No." I shook my head as I felt my future dissolving right in front of me. "I don't, but if you put the gun down . . ." I'd what? Run away with him? Or just let him shoot me and pray he's a horrible shot? "Just . . . calm down."

"You won't leave with me." He sounded so young and confused; more so, he sounded sick and immature.

A few people trickled onto the field behind him, including three of my teammates, and then an eternity passed as Erik watched me. And then I saw Matt, only Matt, his face pale. How was he here? How did he even know I was in trouble? I took a step, time stood still. Was this it? Was I going to die in front of the man I loved just to save him? To save the people who now meant the world to me? "Alright. I'll come with you."

"Great."

God help me. My legs felt like lead as I approached him. "Just put the gun down, alright?"

He dropped his arm to the side.

The gun fell to the ground.

And I remembered Coach Darius's words:

"Kick them twice."

I put my hand on Erik's shoulder and then reared back and kicked him in the nuts as hard as I could, three times, before he fell to the ground. I scrambled for the gun, stood, and towered over him with it aimed where I'd kicked. "Move once and I'm shooting it off."

Sirens sounded around the stadium as a security guard ran toward us, followed by at least six policemen and finally the chief of police in a black suit, looking more ready for an expensive dinner than an arrest and almost homicide. He trained his gun on Erik.

"Erik." Johnny held his hand out for me to stay still. "You're under arrest for the rape of Parker Speedman as well as aggravated assault with a deadly weapon. You have the right to remain silent. Everything you say or do . . ."

I dropped the gun to the ground then sat just as one of the assistant coaches ran over to me. I didn't know him well, but I'd seen him around. He handed me a bottle of water and then showed me his phone. "The only reason I was able to call 911 is because of your bravery in getting his attention away from me. I was so scared for you, for me."

Tears filled my eyes. "Good, that's good."

"That's more than good, sweetheart." He sighed and then just sat next to me on the turf like a good coach would.

He let me cry while he placed a hand on my back and handed me a towel.

And when I saw Matt charging toward me, fear in his eyes, I full-on wept and jumped into his arms.

He held me tight while I cried. Willow was close behind and then suddenly Jagger was there, and Slade with Mack, and what looked like half of the Seattle Sounders team.

"I accidently called the cavalry," Matt whispered in my ear. "Word traveled fast. Willow called Johnny, who was already headed toward the stadium after they looked at the video from the house—it was clearly Erik, and he looked deranged. Johnny had a bad feeling and told us what was happening. Nobody knew who was closest, so everyone just hopped in their cars and drove straight here." He kissed me then, in front of everyone, like I was his, and I clung to him and prayed it would stay like that forever. That we'd never have a reason to be pulled apart or to be ashamed of what we had.

"Fuck you!" Erik yelled as he got cuffed by Johnny. Matt released me and lunged for him, but I stood in front of him.

"Don't," I whispered. "I already got him."

"You shot him? I'm sad I missed that," he said in a stunned voice.

"Worse." Darius walked up and shook his head. "She's a good listener. I advised her to kick him in the balls twice, and she got him three times. Guy puked twice before the police could cuff him."

"I'm sorry you had to even touch him with your foot," Matt growled. "I've never felt so helpless in my entire life watching you out there with him, you were so brave."

Erik turned and tried to glare at us, I grabbed Matt's hand and kissed his face. I wanted Erik to see what real love was.

Because all he wanted was control.

He was a sick bastard, and I wanted to see him locked up.

Still shaking, I walked up to the chief and said, "We can do it here."

"The interview? The confession?"

"I'll tell you everything, but I have one condition."

"What's that?" He grinned. Man, he looked young to be police chief.

"I want to go on camera. I want to tell the world what he did to me. So that girls like me won't be afraid anymore."

He nodded solemnly. "I think I can arrange that," he said. "Go home and rest. If you want a camera crew it might take a few hours or a day to get things situated. I already have your statement that you were raped. It's enough to lock him up, and earlier today one of your teammates, who came from his former team, said she needed to press charges."

I gasped. "Eileen? She said she had an appointment . . ."

He ignored my guess. "Sadly, I think more might come forward, which makes it even more important that you talk about it, so others feel like they have the power as well."

I nodded as Matt wrapped an arm around me. "Let's go home."

"I love our home."

"Me too." He kissed the side of my head. "Me too."

Epilogue

Matt

One month later

"What made you come forward?" Robin Roberts did a great job hosting the interview. Every famous news anchor had begged for the job, but Parker had immediately taken a liking to Robin, something about her being one of Parker's heroes growing up, and it was suddenly easy for Parker to turn every other reporter down. Besides, it was her story and she knew Robin would do an incredible job helping her share it with the world. I smiled as she tugged at her sleek black tank top and crossed her jean-clad legs. The same Valentino shoes I'd gotten her were on her feet for all the world to see. I loved that she went with a mixture of old Parker and new Parker, one that involved allowing me to buy her things like expensive shoes she didn't need. And I loved that she wore them because she wanted a piece of me with her when she was interviewed for the first time.

She looked breathtaking, sexy, confident. I couldn't look away, and I'm sure most of America felt exactly the same. I felt nothing but pride for my girl as she proceeded to answer the question.

"I had a lot of reasons, but mainly, my old agent and now boyfriend, Matt, gave me the strength to speak up, to find my own voice, and to be a role model for other women who may be in the same position—he's everything to me."

And about to be more, she just didn't know it yet.

"Should have worn a dress," Willow grumbled, taking a handful of popcorn while Jagger held the bowl up to her face like he was offering her a popcorn sacrifice and would do anything to stay on her good side.

Parker groaned then covered her face with her hands. "It's so weird seeing myself on TV."

"Get used to it." I wrapped an arm around her and pulled her close, kissing her temple. "Not only are you the star player for the Seattle Reign, but Willow told me you just signed a deal with Adidas?"

Parker beamed up at me. "Weird she may even be a better agent than you?"

Jagger choked on his cough. "You're going to pay for that."

"Oh?" Parker spread her arms wide. "Can't hurt the talent, can you?"

"Who said anything about pain?" I said in a low voice, grabbing her by the arm, tossing her over my shoulder, and marching her into our bedroom, just in time for Jagger to ask loudly if he needed to grab his handy ear plugs.

He exaggerated how much noise we made.

Or so we thought.

And then he bought Willow a matching pair.

Whatever, it was my house and now that renovations were close to being done, I couldn't wait to share all of it with Parker.

Forever.

"You didn't need the dress," I said, setting her on her feet. "The jeans you wore were more you than a dress. You were . . . brilliant." I pressed a heated kiss to her mouth and stepped back, my heart slamming against my ribs.

Her smile fell. "Matt? What's wrong? You look like you're ready to puke."

"Still might happen." I gave my head a shake, turned around in a small circle, patted both pockets, and then just dropped like an idiot to both knees and looked up at her shocked expression. Her cheeks pinked and her hands shook as she covered her mouth.

"Matt?"

The door to my bedroom opened.

Jagger and Willow stood with their phones held high like they were film students, wearing wide grins. My sister's own engagement ring sparkled in the air. Bastard. I was still planning on throwing him off the balcony.

"Parker." My voice shook. "You are the bravest woman I know. You're strong. You're resilient, you're beautiful, talented. It would take me an eternity to tell you all the things I find incredible about you, all the small details that I don't think you even see when you look in the mirror. You are perfected chaos, crazy but in all the ways that make sense to me. I love you." My voice cracked. "Be my wife?"

Her hands fell at her sides as a single tear slid down her cheek, splattering onto the floor. "On one condition."

I frowned up at her. Wasn't prepared for that. "Anything."

She leaned down. "I get the whistle."

I tried to hide my grin and failed. "Open the box."

She hesitated then reached for the blue Tiffany's box, opened it, and burst into tears. "The red whistle!"

"Somehow I figured you needed proof of my love, of my dedication, and I figured it was time you trained me."

Jagger laughed. "Attaboy!"

Willow smacked him in the chest.

"This," Parker sobbed as she pulled me up into her arms, "is the best gift ever, because it's us."

"It is us." I held her tight and then pulled away and reached into my back pocket. "But since Tiffany's wouldn't just sell me a blue box, I got this too."

I held out a single-stone princess-cut ring. I knew Parker wouldn't want something huge, she was an athlete after all, so I went for two karats with perfect clarity.

Another gasp escaped her lips before she launched herself into my arms. "It's perfect."

"The whistle or the ring?"

"Both." She kissed my neck, then grabbed me by the face with both hands, raining kisses all over me until she jumped back and held out her hands. "Now, put the ring on my finger." Apparently I was going too slow because she blew the whistle, followed by, "Take off your pants."

"And that's our cue." Willow laughed, shutting the door quietly behind her and Jagger.

"Seriously?" I faced Parker as she stared at her ring finger and then put the whistle back in her mouth and blew. "Fine! Fine!" I shrugged out of my jeans.

"Wonderful." Parker blew the whistle again. "Ten push-ups."

"Parker, that's not really why I gave you the whistle—"

"Ten push-ups or you're doing burpees. Your choice, Matt." She grinned and then tilted her head like she was seconds away from blowing the whistle again.

"Son of a bitch." I dropped to the ground, did my ten push-ups, then jumped to my feet a bit out of breath.

"I think this is the start to a beautiful marriage." She burst out laughing just as I lunged for her and tossed her onto the bed. The whistle went off at least ten more times before I managed to pry it from her mouth and hands, replacing it with me, my heat, my touch, my kiss.

And then no more whistle. Only us in a tangle of clothes, laughter, and love. Exactly the way it was supposed to be all along.

Acknowledgments

I hate writing these because I always feel like there's someone I forgot, probably because it takes a city to write a book (it really does, especially in this day and age). I'm so thankful to God that I'm able to write every day, that I'm able to create something out of nothing. I would not be here if it weren't for Him.

Thank you to my amazing husband, who's always willing to take the little guy so I can have some extra hours working. He's truly the best husband and my best friend. Thank you, Thor, for understanding that Mama has to work sometimes and that writing books makes it so that you can get fed (my new argument when he asks me to play trains every hour is that I need at least two of those hours to write per day, then we can play trains).

Thank you to Nina at Social Butterfly for ALL THE THINGS, and truly she does all the things, from running ads to just keeping me sane (which I'm sure is more than a full-time job!). To Becca and Jill: You guys are incredible. Thank you from the bottom of my heart. To my admins who run the Rockin' Reader group along with Jill and Ang and everyone else: it always puts a smile on my face to see you guys posting and asking book boyfriend questions! To my beta readers, Tracy, Krista, Georgia, Stephanie, Jill, Candace: Your honesty is always so huge to me. I love that when I ask you to be brutal, you guys don't hold back!

Erica, thank you for always being such a wonderful agent. It just seems to come so natural to you, probably because you are genuinely one of the best people I know. I consider you family, and I'm so happy to have you and Trident behind me.

Maria, my editor, wine friend, and hummus-loving nut: You put a smile on my face every single time we talk. We get each other, and it's always so fun brainstorming with you and working on every project with you and Melody, who is truly one of the best editors around! Which then, of course, makes me think of Kay Springsteen, who looks at every book before I turn it in to make sure that I haven't forgotten to dress my characters. To the entire Skyscape team: you guys are a dream to work with.

To all the bloggers who tirelessly share my books: from the bottom of my heart, thank you.

And to the readers: I don't think words will ever express how thankful I am for your support. You guys make me so happy, not just because you love reading like I do, but because you get just as involved and just as excited. It's such a privilege being a part of this community, so thank you, and I hope you enjoyed Matt and Parker's book!

Hugs, RVD

About the Author

Photo © 2014 Lauren Watson Perry, Perrywinkle Photography

Rachel Van Dyken is a *Wall Street Journal*, *USA Today*, and *New York Times* bestselling author of regency and contemporary romances, including the Red Card novels, *Risky Play* and *Kickin' It*, and her Wingmen Inc. series, which has been optioned for film. A fan of *The Bachelor*, Starbucks coffee, and Swedish fish (not necessarily in that order), Rachel lives in Idaho with her husband and her adorable son. For more information about her books and upcoming events, visit www.RachelVanDykenauthor.com, and follow her on Twitter (@RachVD) and Facebook (@RachelVanDyken).